JURASSIC TOWER

JETHRO WEGENER

SEVERED PRESS
HOBART TASMANIA

JURASSIC TOWER

Copyright © 2021 Jethro Wegener

WWW.SEVEREDPRESS.COM

ISBN: 978-1-922551-80-1

CHAPTER 1

Starling Labs, Midtown Manhattan

Doctor Elizabeth "Lizzie" King was late. This was not a rare occurrence.

A full night of work had seen her pass out in front of her computer sometime in the early morning. She then missed her alarm and had to rush to get ready. New York City's traffic had made sure to get in her way as much as possible, too.

As Lizzie practically fell out of the Uber onto the sidewalk, she struggled to keep hold of her thermos, notebook, handbag, and phone all at once. Thankfully, she'd dressed comfortably in jeans, a t-shirt, and sneakers, so she didn't lose her footing. Instead, she half stumbled before righting herself to hurry forward through the glass doors of Starling Labs.

Located in a towering, glittering skyscraper in the centre of the Midtown Manhattan, Starling Labs had quickly established itself as *the* place to work if you were a biologist, physicist, or almost any other type of scientist. Their funding came from billionaires the world over and had quickly made CERN's budget look small by comparison.

This was why Lizzie couldn't stop her heart pounding as she ran through the lobby. Doctor Waite wouldn't be happy with her, even though he'd been the reason for her massive workload.

She nodded to the security guards on duty as they greeted her, embarrassed that she had yet to learn their names. In an incredible show of acrobatics, Lizzie managed to get her pass card out and tap in without dropping anything. The reader beeped, the gate swung open, and she was into the elevator lobby.

Lizzie could already feel her body crying out for coffee as she jammed the call button. In her bag, she felt her phone vibrating furiously.

Yes, yes! I'm here! she thought impatiently as the elevator started upwards.

Four small screens surrounded her, showing what a great place the lab was to work in. Smiling people in white coats, gloriously modern equipment, and comfortable recreation rooms flashed on-screen as a smooth-voiced narrator sold the place. Lizzie herself had been grabbed by one of the very same ads, but after seeing it about a hundred times a month, the only reaction they got from her these days was an eyeroll.

At last, the elevator doors slid open, revealing the sterile corridor just outside the main physics lab. Behind a marble desk to the left sat more security.

"Doctor Waite is looking for you, Doctor King," said the lady behind the desk.

"Thanks, Janelle," Lizzie said, "and it's Lizzie!"

"Of course, Doctor King," Janelle said with a smile.

Lizzie kept moving, mildly annoyed that Janelle was still so damn formal with her. Not that she had any time to take the lady out for a drink with her schedule, but it still was nice to dream.

Doctor Waite was, predictably, standing by Lizzie's desk when she finally made it. Gym fit, with a heavily frown-lined face, and short dark brown hair, his was not the ideal image for her on that crappy morning.

"Sorry, Doctor Waite," she breathed, putting her stuff down. "I missed my alarm."

He regarded her with his cool blue eyes for a moment. Under his gaze, she withdrew into herself. She knew that he was judging the frizzy red hair, loose t-shirt, and jeans. The man had awfully specific ideas of how "professional women" should dress.

"It's alright, Lizzie," he said at last. "I just wanted to tell you that the work you did for me last night was excellent. In fact, we may be able to put it into action this morning."

Lizzie looked up at him suddenly. "You mean…"

He nodded. "Indeed. It's time to run another test. I wanted to ensure that you'd be here for it. You did a lot of the work for me, after all."

"Of course, Doctor Waite. When?"

Waite looked at his watch, a gold Rolex that was as much a staple of the man's attire as his white lab coat.

"Half an hour."

She nodded. "I'll be there."

"Cool."

Waite looked her up and down once more before leaving, causing a shiver to run down her spine. He'd never tried anything on with her, but Lizzie couldn't help but feel as if his looks were more about undressing her than anything else.

She shook the gaze off of herself. There were more important things to do right now – like get her first cup of coffee. Only once the hot black liquid was steaming away in her mug did Lizzie allow herself a moment to relax.

A sip of the fragrant full-bodied dark roast brought a smile to her face almost immediately. There was very little better than the smooth, dark chocolate flavours of Koa coffee in the morning.

Lizzie closed her eyes, savouring the flavour for a moment, before putting the cup down and pulling on her lab coat. After quickly checking her emails, she grabbed the cup and headed off to the physics lab.

She found Waite and a couple of other scientists that she didn't know very well working hard on the computers in the room. A large sheet of Perspex separated them from the machine on the other side, a hulking science fiction-looking brute of a thing that shone in the florescent light. Thick cables ran into it, providing it with the incredible amounts of power it needed to do its job.

A job that it would finally carry out successfully. Lizzie could barely contain her excitement as she stood in the back, looking at the imposing apparatus that she had helped build. She had to grip the mug firmly in her hands to keep it from shaking.

"Lizzie," Waite said, "can you confirm these calculations?"

Lizzie nodded, moving forward to gaze carefully at the screen in front of her. After a quick run through of the lines, she confirmed that they matched the work she'd done the night before. All except…

"Doctor Waite," she said, pointing with her finger, "that's incorrect, I think."

Waite stepped forward. He examined the equation that her finger was pointing to, but shook his head.

"I had to make a minor adjustment. Otherwise I wouldn't be able to get the desired outcome."

"But Doctor, one wrong line could…"

He silenced her with a wave of his hand, which infuriated her. She clamped her teeth down tight to avoid replying with a cutting response.

"Trust me."

She nodded, stepping back, more to avoid 'accidentally' spilling her scalding hot coffee on him than anything else.

"Are we good to go?" he asked the technicians, who both nodded. "Great! Let's make history."

One of the techs hit a few keys on the computer and the machine started to hum. It slowly increased in intensity as it powered up, going from a low rumble to a bone shaking throb as power coursed through the device. Lizzie's heart hammered in her chest, thudding hard against her ribs like a caged animal fighting for freedom.

In her mug, concentric spirals started forming, starting small and heading to the edge. Soon it was as if her coffee had its own tidal system, waves of the dark liquid spilling out onto the floor as the giant machine seemingly took on a life of its own.

Lizzie was too engrossed in the spectacle that was happening before their eyes to notice the coffee scalding her fingers. A ball of pure energy had started to form just in front of the machine. It shined and undulated like someone had frozen a water droplet in mid-air. The hairs on Lizzie's skin were beginning to stand on-end.

"My god," one of the techs breathed.

"It's working!" Waite exclaimed.

The floor had begun to rumble and the air itself felt like it was charged with electricity. It made everyone's skin tingle pleasantly. Goose pimples had formed on Lizzie's neck and arms. She shuddered, unable to form words or thoughts, so taken was she with the sight in front of her.

The machine was roaring now, a nasty, industrial growl that shook the Perspex shield in its frame. Lizzie's cup fell from her hands, shattering as it hit the floor, the sound of it completely drowned out by the sound of the machine.

The ball of energy was bigger now, about half the size of a man. It no longer resembled clear water as various colours shimmered inside it, giving it the look of an abstract modern art painting.

A computer screen sparked suddenly, exploding outward in a rain of shattered plastic pieces. The tech sitting in front of it was thrown backwards. He let out a yell of surprise as he hit the ground.

"Fuck!" Waite swore, pushing the other tech out of the way. "We need to stop it!"

Lizzie was already on the floor checking on the fallen man. His face was a mass of small cuts that had already started to bleed. He blinked at her in confusion.

It seemed as if the whole building was shaking now, the walls trembling under the pressure, the foundation rattling beneath them. Waite typed away furiously at the computer, struggling to shut it down as the energy ball continued to grow.

Lizzie looked up at it, gasping in surprise. She could have sworn that she saw movement within, graceful shapes slinking around in the tangle of colours. An eye appeared, big and yellow and animalistic. It seemed to lock onto her, staring directly at her from within the orb.

And then it was gone. The room was plunged into pitch blackness, the only sound left behind the heavy breathing of the people in the room. A moment passed. No one spoke. Lizzie's heart continued to thud.

"What the hell?" Waite breathed.

That's when the screaming started.

CHAPTER 2

Kruger National Park, South Africa

The three men stalked through the African bush, exhilarated that they had finally found what they were looking for. Each was dressed in threadbare, dusty clothing that hung loose from their frames. The man in the middle, who was the eldest at thirty-five, carried a rusty Chinese-made knock-off of the Russian AK47 assault rifle.

Their target was a hundred yards in front of them, grazing in the long, khaki grass that spread out across the plains. It was a magnificent rhino, its grey, leathery hide giving it surprisingly effective camouflage.

These men did not care for the animal's beauty, however. Neither did they care that it was endangered. They only had eyes for its horn, which could put food in front of them and their families for a good long while. All they had to do was kill the rhino and hack the horn off of its body.

All three of them had been born in a nearby village, where they had spent their entire lives. Their mothers and fathers had survived the horrors of Apartheid to give birth to them, and they had suffered through years of poverty themselves. By killing this animal, they would be able to at least provide for their wives and children for a little bit longer. Besides, it was not human.

What did an animal's life matter when a man's was at stake?

The man with the rifle was their best shooter. He'd first snuck into the park to hunt game when he was a boy and had only gotten better at it since. He knew exactly where to aim to take the rhino down. Since the animal hadn't noticed the men yet, that made it easier.

He raised the rifle to his shoulder and got the rhino in his sights. Not once had he ever felt remorse at killing animals, and today would be no different.

The wind blew across the bush. Grass and leaves rustled in the breeze. The rhino snorted, continuing to graze happily. It would never know what happened or why. No animal would understand why it was hunted for its prizes.

The man took a breath, moving his finger to the trigger. He made sure that his aim was true once more. His finger started to tighten. A gunshot sounded.

Birds screeched in shock, taking off from their perches. Somewhere in the bush, zebras yelped. The rhino ran off into the trees and was gone in seconds. The three men stood there dumbfounded, because the shot had not come from their rifle.

"Okay, boys," came a voice from behind them, "that was just a warning shot! If you don't want the next one in your head, I'd suggest you drop that weapon."

The men stood frozen to the spot. It was obviously a white man who had spoken, which likely meant that they had been caught by the park rangers. But what puzzled them was that he had spoken in almost perfect *Xhosa*, which was their native language. It was hard for most to grasp, due to the series of clicks that made it so distinctive.

"I will shoot to kill if I have to," the voice said again.

The oldest man dropped his rifle into the dust. A cloud of the stuff was kicked up and quickly swept off by the wind. Around them, the bush had started to quiet down as the animals figured that they had gotten out of danger.

"Great! Now, I want you to take three steps back, put your hands on your head, and interlace your fingers. Then, get on your knees and cross your legs over each other behind you."

The men did as they were told, their hearts pounding and sweat beading on their foreheads. Rangers had permission to kill poachers on-sight. Was this man going to execute them?

Getting down on their knees was awkward with their hands on their heads. They wobbled a bit, almost faceplanting in the dirt, before managing it. Sand scraped against their cargo pants as they crossed their legs over behind them. The unpleasant sound and texture of it against their skin made them shiver.

There they waited, fear creeping into their hearts. They heard no sound from behind them. Somewhere in the trees, a Go Away Bird warned a herd that there was a predator nearby. It wasn't until their hands were pulled roughly behind their backs and zip tied that they saw the man who had gotten the drop on them.

He was a tall white man in khaki clothing, boots, and a bush hat. His skin was tanned and leathery, making his rugged face appear older than it was. A neatly trimmed salt and pepper beard went into short, greying dark blonde hair. His eyes were a piercing grey that pinned the men to the spot with their gaze.

They watched him, the plastic zip ties digging uncomfortably into their skin, as he keyed a radio on his chest. He held a rifle in his right hand with the casual ease of one who had used such a weapon all his life.

"Themba," the man said into his radio, "this is De Vries here. I got three *okes* here ready to be taken in."

"Where are you?" came the reply.

"Just head east from where you are for a couple of Ks," De Vries said, "you'll find me."

"Alright, Dante," Themba replied, "we'll be there soon."

"Roger that," De Vries said. "Right, now that my friends are on their way, I just want to let you *okes* know that you have a choice. Do you want to know what it is?"

The oldest man looked up at his captor. The other two kept their heads down, not wanting to say anything that would get them killed.

"What choice?" the oldest asked.

"Between jail and school, my friend," De Vries said with a smile.

He cast a glance about him, spying a rock that was just the right height. He walked over to it and sat down, his rifle laid across his knees.

"You see," he said, pulling a bright red apple out of one pocket and a knife out of the other, "I don't want to have to kill you. It's just a waste of life, hey? I'd much rather you joined my guys."

The oldest captive laughed. "Join you? As what? Cook boys?"

De Vries grimaced at the last phrase. He cut himself a bit of apple and crunched on it thoughtfully.

"No, nothing like that. I want you three to join the rangers. I've been following you for quite some time. You're all good trackers. Bloody good. It's a paid position, we'll give you the training you need. All you have to do is sign a contract."

The men looked at him suspiciously. "Are you telling the truth?"

"Of course, man!" He offered them a slice of apple, which each refused. "I wouldn't waste my time talking to you if I were lying. Themba will fill you in when he gets here. He's my friend and the one in command of the unit."

The three men discussed among themselves for a minute in hushed tones. De Vries understood every word, but he kept quiet, cutting slices off his apple, and crunching on them slowly. Once he'd reached the core, the men seemed to have come to a decision. He chucked the apple core into the bush.

"You promise this is real?"

De Vries nodded. "Paid, legal, and reliable. I know you *okes* have families. I'll do my best to make sure you get paid a fair wage. I'm the only white man in the unit if that matters. Your orders will come from Themba, not me."

"You'll let us think about this?"

"Of course. When Themba gets here–"

The thumping of helicopter blades in the air cut his sentence short. De Vries looked up, seeing a dark black chopper flying straight for them. He hefted his rifle, unsure what was going on.

The helicopter landed in a clearing about fifty feet away, kicking up a huge cloud of dust and loose, dry vegetation that swirled around in the vortex created by its rotors. De Vries shut his eyes tight against the grit.

A fit young woman in a black suit climbed out and jogged towards De Vries. She was a little over five foot six, gym fit, with short black hair, and a dark complexion. As she came to a halt in front of him, he noticed that her eyes were a striking hazel colour.

"Dante De Vries?" she asked, her accent marking her as American.

De Vries eyed her warily. "Who's asking?"

"Special Agent Alexa Rojas," the woman said, holding out her hand. "My agency needs your help. It's a matter of life and death, Mr. De Vries."

CHAPTER 3

The helicopter flew low over the savannah, giving the impression that one could just reach out and touch the tops of the trees as they sped past. De Vries sat across from Alexa, watching her carefully. Each had a large, cumbersome headset on so that they could communicate over the roar of the rotors.

"We need you to sign this," Alex said, handing De Vries a document attached to a clipboard.

He looked it over. It was a confidentiality agreement, of sorts. Underneath it was a contract.

"I'd need to read this first."

Alexa nodded. "As long as you sign the damn thing. We need you on this job."

"Why me?"

"Because you're one of the best rangers we can find, and you have armed forces experience."

De Vries grimaced. His time in the South African Army had been long ago. It was a period he'd rather forget.

"Can you tell me what the job is before I sign?"

Alexa eyed him for a moment, then turned to the pilot. She made a cut off sign with her hand. The man nodded, reached up, and flicked a switch.

"It's only you and me on this channel," the agent said, leaning forward in her seat. "What I have to tell you is confidential, so you need to promise you'll sign that."

"You have my word," De Vries said, holding out his hand.

They shook, her grip firm and strong. If he'd been a lesser man, it would have intimidated him.

"Twenty-four hours ago, Starling Labs in New York City went into lockdown," Alexa said. "An alarm was sounded within the building. It alerted us."

"Never heard of the place."

"They're working on some cutting-edge tech, as well as some less than savoury things. I don't have all the details, but my agency has been monitoring them for some time. We've been gathering intel to raid the place. Then, something happened. The place shut down. It's a fortress, almost impossible to get into. Our only choice is to go in through the roof."

"What's your agency?"

"Let's just say that we keep an eye on companies like Starling. Mega corporations that have unlimited funding and no scruples. We have a team of highly trained soldiers standing by to breach. Whatever is in there could be incredibly dangerous."

"I still don't see where I come in."

"Our intel has it that there are live animals in the building."

"Don't most labs work with rats and monkeys?" De Vries asked.

"I'm not talking about the usual fare," Alexa said, "I'm talking lions, and tigers, and bears."

"Oh my."

CHAPTER 4

Unnamed Hotel, Midtown Manhattan

Alexa rubbed the sleep from her eyes as the helicopter – the third she had taken in twenty-four hours – cut through the air above Manhattan. Her phone was buzzing in her pocket, the incessant vibrations against her leg having roused her from her fitful sleep. Across from her, De Vries dozed.

She pulled it out. It was a message from her son, checking in on her. Alexa smiled, tapped off a quick reply, and shoved the phone back in her pocket.

"That's the first smile I've seen from you," De Vries said.

Alexa looked up to see his eyes on her. They sparkled in a way that she had read about in books, but never actually seen.

"My son," she said by way of explanation.

He nodded. "How old?"

"Just turned twelve last month."

"Coming up on the teenage years."

"I know. I keep wondering if it will be as bad as they say."

De Vries smiled. "For some, it is. For others, it's a piece of piss."

"That... doesn't sound much better."

He laughed, deep and hearty. "You'll find out, soon enough."

"Two minutes!" came the pilot's voice over the headset.

Alexa acknowledged, before leaning forward. She pointed out the window at a massive glass behemoth that stood tall and proud among the other skyscrapers.

"That's Starling Labs!"

"*Jisslaaik*," De Vries breathed. "A company built that?"

"Renovated. You'd be surprised how much money these pharma companies have in the bank."

"And where is our objective?"

"The lower floors," Alexa said. "Although that's our best guess. We can't actually find accurate information on what's inside that thing."

"Starling sounds like a bunch of crooks!"

"That's why my agency has been watching them! Nothing adds up."

The chopper touched down on a rooftop landing pad, the impact jarring its occupants slightly. Alex pulled off her headset and slid the door open. Lieutenant Mykelti Monroe stood at the edge of the pad, his urban camo BDUs being buffeted by the downdraft.

"Good flight, ma'am?" he asked when the copter had powered down,

"Long," Alexa replied. "Dante De Vries meet Lieutenant Mykelti Monroe. He's the military team lead on this op."

He was just shorter than De Vries, with deep set black eyes, a wide nose, and a bald head. He held out his hand and the two men shook.

"Your team ready?" Alexa asked.

They were headed down the metal stairs of the landing pad, towards a door into the building. De Vries had just realised that they had landed on the roof of a fancy hotel. A red carpet led from the pad to the door.

"Yes, ma'am," Monroe replied, pushing open the doors. "We're ready to go when you are. Unless you need a nap first."

The corners of Alexa's mouth turned upward. "Wake your men from theirs, Lieutenant. We're on the clock here."

"Yes, ma'am."

"And stop calling me ma'am."

The red carpet continued inside, leading straight to an elevator with brass doors. They were scrupulously clean, De Vries noted as he hit the call button.

"You ex-South African Army?" Monroe asked as they stepped inside.

De Vries nodded. "During Apartheid, yes. Not our finest moment."

Monroe grunted. "I know. I remember the stickers and fridge magnets we had around the house as a kid. And Pieter Vorstedt, of course."

"That movie didn't get to us until a while after the regime finally crumbled."

"I wonder why?"

The elevator dinged, the doors opening to reveal a corridor. Alexa led the way, heading straight for a set of ornate double doors. She pushed them open to reveal a grand ballroom, with a delicately painted high ceiling that seemed to stretch on forever.

Inside, people were scrambling. Phones rang incessantly, multiple screens showed multiple news channels, and the buzz of activity was loud enough to disturb the dead. Alexa's agency had taken control of a hotel and set up a command centre in their ballroom. De Vries wondered if the plush red carpet would survive the constant scurrying about.

Alexa strode through the chaos, people parting before her without being asked. They were heading towards a big oak table in the centre of the room. It was stacked with all kinds of military kit.

Monroe's men were gathered around it, checking their gear, making sure everything was good to go for the operation. They had no idea what they would be walking into, so they were equipped with the standard gear for an urban environment, including rifles, sidearms, body armour, and comms.

"This our great white hunter?" Specialist Mike Teller asked.

De Vries docked his bush hat to the group and nodded. "Seems so."

"Don't see why we need a hunter on this," Specialist Ashan Khan said.

"Do you want to be the one to deal with the fucking tigers?" asked Specialist "Peanut" Jacoby. "Cause I ain't gonna be taking on no fucking tiger."

"Yeah, your scrawny ass wouldn't last five minutes," Ashan replied.

"Hey! I give myself even odds at lasting seven."

"Cut the chatter!" Monroe commanded and the men fell silent.

Introductions were made. Teller was the tallest, but only slightly, bearded, with a handsome, TV-star like face and dark hair. Next to him was Ashan, a man with a dark complexion, hazel eyes, and a neatly trimmed black beard.

Last up was Peanut, a short man that seemed to be mostly muscle, a crooked, oft broken nose, and brown eyes that sat in a heavily lined, and scarred square face.

Alexa grabbed a bag from under the table and handed it to De Vries.

"Your kit. Bathroom over there. Time to get your asses moving, gentlemen. We're Oscar Mike in fifteen."

As De Vries jogged to the bathroom, Monroe watched him go.

"You sure about him, ma'am?"

Alexa nodded. "He wouldn't be here if I weren't. And stop calling me ma'am or I'm going to deck you, Lieutenant."

With that she grabbed her own bag and headed off after De Vries.

"You trust him, sir?" Teller asked, slipping into his body armour.

"You heard the lady," Monroe replied. "Now cut the chatter and get kitted up. Clock's ticking."

CHAPTER 5

The copter soared over the deserted streets towards Starling Labs, Alexa sitting next to the pilot. De Vries was in the back with the military guys, taking in the sights as they flew past the window, this being his first time in the city.

The four military men were fully kitted up in camo, body armour, and helmets. Each was carrying an FN SCAR 17S assault rifle, a favourite of the U.S. Special Operations Command. De Vries had his own weapon, a Remington R-25 chambered for .308 Winchester rounds, which Alexa had helped him bring into the country.

"I'll tell you, brother," Teller said, "I don't feel too good about this one."

"Worried about the animals?" Peanut asked, chuckling. "I'm sure our weapons will put 'em down pretty quick."

Teller shook his head. "Just don't feel right."

"How many times we been out?" Monroe asked.

"A fair few," Teller said with a sigh.

"Come on, Mike," Ashan said, patting his knee, "I'll read you a bedtime story about a princess later."

"Don't know those princess books, my man," Teller said with a smile. "My daughter and son fall right asleep every time."

"You read to them, I read to you?"

"Sure thing, brother. Just gotta promise to cuddle up real close."

Ashan laughed. "Your wife won't mind?"

"Nope. She knows I love you boys."

Peanut laughed. "Can I come?"

"You'd just ruin the mood with your face, Peanut," Monroe said. "Bad enough I have to look at it every damn day. Don't make me see it in my dreams and in bed too."

"This, sir," Peanut said, reaching up and running his hand over his face, "is called rugged handsomeness. I may not be as pretty as Mike, but I sure get my fair share of attention."

"Yeah, when they throw you out the place," Ashan said with a laugh.

"That only happened once, bro! And if I recall, you didn't back me up."

"Hey, I was drinking a very nice non-alcoholic soda. Besides, they were some big dudes."

The four men laughed. Even De Vries and Alexa found themselves smiling. He missed the banter from when he was in the army. It was about the only thing he really missed. He stretched his leg out, massaging it slightly. The ache had started.

Finally, the roof of the labs came into view. A helipad had been painted on the massive flat surface, presumably for use by CEOs and investors. As soon as the chopper touched down, Monroe slid open the door and his men were out.

De Vries was right behind them as they cleared the roof and hoofed it to the entry to the building. Alexa tapped the pilot on the shoulder, before jumping out and waving him off. She was carrying a Sig-P226 handgun.

Monroe cast a glance to Alexa, who nodded. Monroe gave the breaching order. Peanut stepped up to the door, tried it first, then set a breaching charge. Everyone stepped back, turning their faces away, as Peanut triggered the charge.

There was a muffled whump, a spray of water, and the steel door was blown inwards in a shower of debris. Moving with graceful precision, Monroe and his men entered the building through the still smoking doorway, sweeping the small reception area beyond for any threats.

"Clear!" Monroe called from inside.

Alexa went in first, then De Vries. Inside, all looked normal. A reception desk sat directly in front of the door, elevators to the right and a stairwell to the left. The area was lit by the pale glow of emergency lighting, and apart from the ruined door on the floor, everything was in order.

"Computers are down," Teller said from behind the desk. "No juice in these things, man."

"Whole place must be on backup power," Alexa said. "I'm guessing they'd prioritise the labs over all other electronics."

"Damn elevator's down," Peanut declared.

"Not like we were gonna take it anyway," Ashan said.

Alexa pulled out a hardwearing phone and checked their location. "Next five floors are offices. Then we get into blacked out territory on all public records. I'm guessing that's where they're hiding the labs."

"You *okes* thinking terrorists?"

Alexa nodded. "Who knows what weapons these guys could have been developing with their budget. Makes sense someone would want to steal it."

De Vries made a noncommittal noise. Something felt off about this whole operation, but he couldn't put his finger on what it was.

"Okay then," Monroe said, "stairs it is. Stay behind us, but keep close."

Monroe and his men stacked up at entry to the stairwell. Peanut went first, then Ashan. They swept the area before calling back that it was clear.

"Sweep and clear all floors?" the lieutenant asked Alexa.

She nodded. "Double time."

Monroe acknowledged, tapped Teller on the shoulder, and the four military guys went down the stairs to the next floor. Alexa and De Vries followed. De Vries grunted as he made his way down.

"You okay?" Alexa asked.

He nodded. When she wasn't looking, he slipped his hand into his pocket. He pulled out a pill and quickly swallowed it before anyone noticed.

The two watched Monroe and his men stack up once more, then enter the next floor. As they went, De Vries peeked through the doorway. It was a dark office that seemed to stretch on forever, divided into low cubicles. He couldn't even see the other end, giving him some idea of the scale of the building he was in.

He noticed that the windows were all shuttered, something dull just visible underneath the glass. De Vries peered at it for a moment, trying to discern what it was in the low light.

"Lockdown procedure," Alexa commented. "When the system detects signs of trouble, titanium plates slide down over every inch of this building."

"I guess we're sealed up tight."

"Yep. That's why we came in through the roof. Only soft access point."

Monroe and his men were on their way back.

"Any intel?" Alexa asked.

The lieutenant shook his head. "It's weird. Everything is powered down, even the laptops. Looks like there was some commotion, but not a lot up here."

"Looks more like someone pulled the fire alarm by accident," Ashan observed. "People just calmly stopped what they were doing and started down the stairs. Not even any phones left lying around."

"Okay, we keep going. Lead the way, Monroe."

The process was repeated on the next floor. The stack up, the entry, the room sweep. Except this time, everything was different.

CHAPTER 6

"Jesus," Peanut breathed.

The veteran of two tours felt bile rise in his throat. Hot, acidic, nasty. It stung. He blinked, hoping against hope that his eyes were playing tricks on him. But they weren't.

There was blood *everywhere*. On the floor, the walls, coating the insides of cubicles, smeared all over the windows. It had dried a dark brown, but the stench of it hadn't left the room. It was almost overpowering, the coppery smell of it, the way it got stuck in the back of their throats, making them taste it.

Teller wretched. But the men kept their composure. They moved forward, rifles up, each covering their assigned space.

Each saw their share of the horror. Limbs were scattered about like there had been an explosion in a doll factory. None were severed clean. They all ended in ragged flesh, ripped from bodies without mercy.

Ashan's foot touched something. He looked down to see a woman's head, eyes open and staring in horror, as it rolled away from him. Hair trailed behind it, sticky and matted with the owner's blood. He said a prayer to Allah under his breath, hoping the woman found peace.

They finally reached the end of the floor. Monroe was breathing through his mouth by this point, the smell too much, even for him. As he walked back to Alexa, he tried to keep his eyes off the carnage that surrounded him, but it was everywhere.

"What do you think, Dante?" Alexa asked.

De Vries had crouched next to a cubicle. An arm and a leg were in there, the leg propped up against the computer. He pulled out his knife, using it to move the limbs without touching them.

"This sure as shit wasn't terrorists, my friends," he announced. "Look here, and here. Bite marks. Definitely animal. Look at the way the skin is torn. Only a predator's teeth can do that. And here, on this leg, you see that long, jagged cut? That's from some sort of claw."

"Let me get this straight," Peanut said, "you're telling us that a fucking tiger did this?"

De Vries stood. He shook his head.

"I don't know what did this, but it probably wasn't a tiger. The bite patterns are wrong."

"Best guess?" Alexa asked.

De Vries shrugged. "I'd need to examine more of this stuff to see. It's odd though. Why so many dead? Why all the carnage? A predator is more likely to pick off a kill, then take it away to eat it. Not just go mad like this."

"You sure about that?" Monroe asked. "Surely an animal doesn't think. It just sees meat."

"*Ja*, I'm sure, man. Take lions, like the *Tsavo Man-Eaters*, they pick off one at a time. They don't hunt for sport. They hunt to eat. Unless…"

"Unless what?"

"It could be that whatever animal did this was overly aggressive, confused maybe. Even then, all of this? It's a bit of a stretch."

"Great!" Peanut exclaimed. "Our expert don't know shit!"

"Shut it," Alexa commanded. "We don't have time to examine all the dead. We need to keep clearing floors."

De Vries walked over to the stairwell. He leaned over the railing, looking down, paying particular attention to the steps themselves.

"There's something else," he said. "No blood on the stairs."

"What difference does that make, man?" Teller asked.

"It means that unless whatever did this came up in the bloody lift, how the hell did it get up here? And perhaps more importantly, where did it go?"

"It doesn't matter how it got here," Monroe said, "but where it went could be a problem. Keep your eyes and ears open, and pucker those buttholes. We got hostiles."

"I told you I didn't feel good about this one, brother," Teller said, shaking his head.

Ashan said a prayer in Arabic. Peanut gave him a look.

"Hope your God has our backs, bro."

"He does. Although whatever did this isn't from Him."

"Abandon hope, all ye who enter here," De Vries said.

"Bit cliché, don't you think?" Alexa asked.

He shrugged. "Seemed appropriate."

"Come on, let's get moving, ladies and gents," Monroe said.

As the guys went through to clear the next floor, DeVries kept going down the stairs. He came up against a makeshift barricade of filing cabinets, chairs, and random pieces of office equipment. He was sure that the paper strewn over the blockade wasn't going to do much, but panic makes people do weird things.

"Alexa," De Vries called.

"Son of a bitch," she swore when she saw what he was looking at.

"Are you thinking what I am?"

She nodded. "This barricade came from upstairs. How did the animal get through to them?"

"Clear up here!"

De Vries and Alexa jogged up the stairs. The office was a duplicate of the other three, except that this one was missing a lot of furniture. Sheets of paper were strewn about the floor, a few computers had been knocked over, but other than that, there weren't any signs of violence.

"So, they barricaded the stairs and went upstairs to die?" Teller asked. "That doesn't make sense. Why not head to the roof and lock themselves up there?"

"Maybe they felt safe behind the barricade?" De Vries suggested.

"That's not our main problem," Alexa said. "Two more floors to go before we get to the labs. We need to get past the blockage."

"I have an idea," Ashan said.

They followed him as he walked over to the bank of elevators that was set in just outside the office. He chose an elevator, then examined it for a moment. His eyes fixed on a small hole on the upper right side of the doors.

"I can get us through these," he said.

Monroe nodded. Ashan pulled a tool from out of his vest pocket. It was a long piece of metal, hinged at one end. He jammed it into the hole. There was a metallic clunk as the hinged part of the key formed a 90-degree angle, and a *thunk* as Ashan turned the key.

"Where in the hell did you get one of those?" Peanut asked.

"It's called a drop key," Ashan said, shoving it back in his pocket. "I was on an op once where half my team got trapped in the damn elevator. Been carrying one ever since."

Teller pulled the doors open. They slid back easily, revealing an empty elevator shaft.

"How'd they get out?" Peanut asked.

"With great difficulty. We were a laughing stock for some time after that."

Peanut chuckled. "Not gonna lie, bro, that's pretty funny."

"There's a ladder in the shaft," Teller said, pointing it out. "If we're careful, we can climb down."

"Looks like we're climbing, ladies and gents," Monroe said.

Then they heard it. A long, low howl that sent tendrils of dread creeping into their hearts. It came up the shaft, echoing off the walls, making it sound almost spectral by the time it reached their ears. It went on for half a minute before fading, leaving nothing behind but the horror of its memory.

Peanut looked down the shaft. "That ain't no fucking tiger."

CHAPTER 7

All eyes turned to De Vries.

"Don't look at me," he said, "I haven't a *fokken* clue what that was."

"It sounded big, whatever it is," Teller said, turning to Monroe. "I told you, brother. Shit show."

Monroe stared down the shaft thoughtfully. "Let's get to the labs. If something comes at you, kill it. Clear?"

Everyone nodded. De Vries looked uncomfortable.

"Problem?"

"I don't like killing," he replied, hefting his rifle. "This is a last resort in my business."

"You must be a hell of a hunter, then," Monroe said sarcastically. "Peanut, Ashan, you two go first. Then Alexa and De Vries. Teller, with me."

"Got it, boss" Peanut said.

He grabbed the rungs of the ladder and swung himself into the shaft. For a brief second, he felt weightless, as if he could float gently to the ground without any trouble. Then it was gone as gravity decided to make itself known once more. He started down. Ashan followed.

"How do I get the door open?" Peanut called up when he arrived on the right floor.

"There's a mechanism above the door," Ashan said, "just release it! It's a clutch of sorts that keeps the doors locked."

Peanut found what Ashan mentioned, a complicated system of metal and wheels and pulleys. He examined it for a moment, figured out how to open it, then reached out and released it.

With one hand gripping the side of the ladder firmly, he reached out with his other. He pushed his fingertips into the gap between the doors and started to pull. His heart thudded in his chest. Sweat started to bead on his forehead.

Peanut pulled, hard. The door gave easier than he had expected, sliding towards him so fast that he was pushed back. For one brief, horrifying moment he was hanging from the ladder with only one hand, the other dangling out into empty space.

"Got you, brother," Ashan said.

He grabbed the back of Peanut's and held tight until his comrade could right himself. Peanut hugged the ladder for a moment, breathing hard.

"Fuck me, bro, I owe you one," Peanut exclaimed.

"Just get your dumb ass through those doors so that I can get my feet on solid ground again!"

"Amen, bro."

Peanut stepped off the ladder as quickly as he dared to, finding himself in a sterile white corridor. He brought his weapon to his shoulder and swept the hall.

"Clear!" he called.

Ashan landed next to him. The two men went down the hall, Peanut sweeping left and Ashan right. There were two doors in the hallway, one all the way at the end, and another marked 'Rec Room' halfway down on the right.

Ashan tried the door and found it locked. He knocked.

"U.S. Military!" he called, standing back from the door just in case.

Silence. He nodded to Peanut, and they continued to the door at the end of the corridor. It was locked up tight, a numerical keypad set in the wall beside it. The two men jogged back to the shaft and called for the others to come down.

Alexa arrived first. De Vries found himself struggling. His leg was starting to go from a dull ache to a searing pain. He'd taken his painkiller too late to stop it. A cold sweat had broken out across his body.

"You okay, De Vries?" Teller asked, noticing how much the older man was battling.

De Vries nodded, his mouth dry. All he had to do was make it down a few more rungs and he was there. He stepped down, placing his weight gingerly on his sore leg. Pain shot up from his thigh immediately. It was so bad that it paralysed him. His left hand lost its grip and he almost fell into the abyss.

Teller acted fast, bracing his legs against the ladder and snatching at De Vries' hand. The two men held on tight, De Vries' fall stopping suddenly, causing him to grunt. Monroe was already calling to Alexa and the others.

A slow rumbling started suddenly. It came up through the ladder first, causing the steel to vibrate beneath Teller's grip. Then the walls started to shake. Alexa, Peanut, and Ashan were thrown off their feet as the floor shifted beneath them.

Teller lost his grip, slipping off the ladder in the process. As he and De Vries fell, Monroe made a desperate grab for them. But as another quake hit the building, he was falling too. Time seemed to slow for the three of them, as if they were floating in mid-air.

Alexa saw the three of them fall past her floor as she was running to help. She looked down the shaft, a horrified expression on her face, a word on her lips that never made it out.

As they fell, sparks started around them. Bright blue flashes of what looked like lightning zapped the air. Alexa watched as a floating orb formed below the three men, an undulating ball of energy that sparkled and fizzed and crackled.

De Vries was the first one to hit it. Alexa had expected screaming, blood, and maybe an explosion, but the man just disappeared. Teller was next, followed closely by Monroe, and then the ball was gone as suddenly as it had appeared.

It left nothing behind expect the floaters and flashers that had burned themselves into Alexa's vision.

CHAPTER 8

One minute, they were falling through darkness, and the next, there was light. Brilliant. White. Blinding. De Vries shut his eyes tight against it. A moment later, he landed hard in the dirt. A cloud of dust kicked up around him.

Teller landed on De Vries. Both men grunted at the impact as they had the wind knocked out of them. A foot to their right, Monroe hit, a swear word escaping his mouth as he did so.

The three men lay there in silence for a moment, struggling to breathe. The sun blasted down on them, hot and unforgiving. Creatures called, growled, and sang their various songs. Off in the far distance, something roared.

De Vries gently pushed a groaning Teller off of him. He sat up slowly, squinting about, trying to get his bearings. The air smelled different to any other he had ever smelled. It was fresher, but with a hint of something else that he couldn't quite place.

"Teller," De Vries said, looking at the man, "you okay?"

"That *fucking* hurt," Teller breathed. "You're a solid motherfucker."

De Vries laughed. "Any idea where we are?"

Teller looked about. "Not where we started, that's for sure."

Desert scrubland stretched off into the distance all around them. Strange plants dotted the hard-packed dirt landscape at odd intervals. The sun was merciless, so hot that it felt as if De Vries was cooking in his vest.

Monroe stood up on shaky legs. He used the scope on his rifle to scan the horizon.

"How in the hell did we get here?" he asked.

De Vries noticed that the hairs on the back of his arms were standing up. He checked with Teller and Monroe. Same story.

"I'm no scientist, my friends," he said, "but I'd say we fell through a portal of some kind."

"What? Like from some science fiction movie?" Teller asked incredulously.

"*Ja.*"

"And how would you know that?" Monroe asked.

De Vries stood up. He dusted himself off.

"Because I read a lot of science fiction Always been my favourite genre."

Monroe grunted. "In the absence of anything else, I guess that makes you our expert."

"I don't really care how we got here," Teller said. "How we gonna get ourselves back?"

Off in the distance, something roared. It sounded big, the roar carrying across the empty space towards them. The three men immediately had their rifles up, their eyes scanning for the creature. Neither could shake the feeling that the howl had sounded hungry.

Then the air started to crackle around them. De Vries was the first to notice. The hairs on his arms were standing on end, goose pimples crisscrossing his skin. He was about to call out when they were engulfed in another ball of energy.

All three of them yelled in surprise, the ground they were standing on no longer there anymore. De Vries felt his stomach lurch upwards, as if he was on a roller coaster, and they were falling again.

Thankfully, it wasn't from such a great height this time.

They hit the floor soon after, the impact knocking their brains around in their skulls. De Vries cried out in agony, his leg taking much of the impact. Teller landed on his tailbone, a jolt of white-hot pain shooting through his spine to his head, making him see stars.

Monroe was the first one up. He brought his rifle to his shoulder and did a three-sixty of the room, sweeping for threats.

Dim light illuminated their new surroundings. Pale, orange, artificial. The floor was sterile white tiles, the walls around them the same. Beakers, test tubes, and other glass receptacles lined the walls. Complicated looking equipment, all steel and hard lines and buttons, was dotted about the place.

De Vries hauled himself to his feet, gritting his teeth against the pain. Teller used a nearby table to help himself up.

"Looks like we don't have to worry about getting back anymore, my China," De Vries said.

Movement in the corner caught his eye.

"Movement!" he called, aiming his weapon at what he'd seen. "This is the U.S. Military! We are here to help! Show yourself slowly, with your hands up."

By now, Monroe and Teller both had their SCAR rifles aimed at the same place. Silence descended upon the lab. Nothing moved for a second, until, slowly, a pair of hands emerged from behind a table.

"Don't shoot," said a female voice, "I'm friendly!"

"Come out slowly, with your hands in the air," Monroe commanded.

A woman with a buzz cut and an angular face juxtaposed with a delicate nose, stood up, her hands raised high. She was wearing what looked like a security uniform over her lean, muscular frame.

"Janelle Miller, sir," the woman said, "security for the building. My ID badge is pinned to my vest. Gun on my right hip."

"You ex-military, Miss Miller?"

Janelle nodded. "Marines."

"Semper Fi, sister," Teller said.

Monroe approached Janelle warily. He got close enough to read her ID badge, then nodded, lowering his rifle.

"You guys MARSOC or something?" Janelle asked, putting her hands down.

"Or something," Teller said.

"What's the situation, Marine?" Monroe asked.

"No idea, sir," Janelle said. "Power went out, building started to shake, and some real weird shit's been happening ever since."

"Like energy portals?" De Vries asked.

"Yeah. Screaming too. Heard some gunshots. I was trying to clear the building, then the damn lab doors shut. I've been stuck in here since."

"Terror attack?" Monroe said.

"Honestly, sir? No fucking idea. You ask me, terrorists would have gone floor by floor to clear the building, if they were smart. Maybe gone straight to the labs to get what they were after. I'd have heard more shots. But instead, I've been hearing…"

"Animal sounds," De Vries finished.

Janelle nodded. "Freaked me the fuck out, man. And I did two tours in the suck."

"How do we get out of this lab?" Monroe asked.

Janelle pointed to a heavy-looking steel door. Solid, imposing, formidable. It shone dully in the dim light.

"Only way out, sir."

Teller stared at the door for a moment.

"For fuck's sake, it just ain't our fucking day, is it?"

CHAPTER 9

"What the hell just happened?" Peanut asked, staring down the elevator shaft in disbelief.

Alexa stood next to him, just as dumbfounded. The air still crackled with energy. A strong smell of burnt ozone filled the air.

"Do you think they're dead?" Ashan asked.

"They just fell into a goddamn energy ball, bro. I don't know what to think!"

Alexa keyed her radio. "Monroe, De Vries, Teller, respond."

Silence. She tried another couple of times. There was no reply.

"Okay," she said after a moment of thought, "unless we see proof to contrary, they're alive. We continue with the mission. Am I clear?"

The two soldiers nodded, although Peanut hesitated first. Alexa gave him a look, trying to read his body language. Her years in the FBI had taught her a lot about reading people and she didn't want to lose these men. Eventually, he nodded once more.

"Guess you're in charge, ma'am," he said.

"Don't call me ma'am and we'll get along just fine," Alexa said. "Now, let's get this door open."

Alexa pulled her phone out of her pocket, tapped away at the screen for a moment, then keyed a number into the electronic keypad. Ashan and Peanut took up positions on either side of the door. She nodded, and pressed enter on the keypad. The door whooshed up, sounding like it was from a video game, and Alexa stepped back as they swept past her into the room beyond.

Just as Ashan was about to call 'clear', the building was shaking once more. Peanut almost lost his footing. He reached out and steadied himself using a lab table. All around them, glass containers jangled in their housing.

"Clear!" Peanut called when the shaking had stopped.

Alexa entered the room, discovering a biological lab. Beakers and equipment were everywhere, and further down was what looked to be a hermitically sealed door. The word 'Biohazard' was printed on it in big, angry red letters.

"You think the building will be able to take all these tremors, ma– Alexa?" Ashan asked.

"That's the least of our worries," she said, examining the equipment around them. "If that door over there is anything to go by, Starling was working on some dodgy stuff."

"In the middle of the city?" Peanut asked. "Seems dangerous to me."

"I don't think Starling care. Or maybe they just needed to be connected to the Manhattan power grid."

Ashan stood in front of the 'Biohazard' door. He shivered, thinking of all the people in the offices around them. All that was needed to kill millions was one slip-up or careless janitor.

"How far back have we pushed the cordon?" he asked.

Alexa looked up. "Maybe not far enough."

Their radios crackled to life. "This is Lieutenant Monroe. Alexa, Ashan, Peanut, do any of you copy?"

"Alexa here. Glad to hear your voice, Lieutenant. We feared the worst. What happened?"

"De Vries reckons interdimensional portal. Best we got, so let's go with it for now. We found a survivor."

"Any solid intel?"

"Not much, except that this might not be terrorists."

"Well, we've just discovered that they've been working on biohazardous material up here."

"Shit, do we need to call in the RRT from the CDC?"

"No. Not yet. Seems sealed up tight. What floor you on?"

"Couple down from you, apparently. Orders?"

Alexa considered their options. "Keep moving down, if you can. Keep us advised. We need to hurry. I don't like these tremors."

"Roger that. Monroe out."

"What do we do about this?" Peanut asked, gesturing to the door.

"We leave it. Our main objective right now is to get actionable intel. Once we have that, we can send in the RRT guys."

Peanut shivered. "Yeah, let the dudes in the monkey suits deal with the potentially deadly diseases. Good plan."

They went back out into the hallway, sealing the door behind them.

It really does sound like it's from those video games my son plays, but which one? Starts with a 'D' I think...

She shook the thought from her head, although she knew it would bug her. For the first time in Alexa's life, she was glad that she didn't have the money for a fancy Manhattan apartment. She didn't want Lucas anywhere near this.

"Your turn to go first, Ashan," Peanut said. "You got God on your side. You'll be fine."

Ashan grunted, slung his rifle, and swung out onto the ladder. Once he was climbing, Peanut did the same, followed by Alexa. All three gripped the ladder in a vice-like grip with the threat of another tremor hanging over their heads.

Upon reaching the next floor, Ashan unlocked the doors, slid them open, and hopped out into the corridor beyond. A security desk was to his right, an office at the end of the hallway he was in. There were no threats visible, so he called the others down.

"You hear that?" Alexa asked.

All three listened hard. There it was. It sounded as if someone was methodically banging on a heavy door.

"Morse code," Ashan said. "S.O.S."

The two soldiers moved first, each taking a side of the space as they moved. Alexa remained a few steps behind, her weapon ready while observing trigger discipline and letting the men do their job.

They cleared the office first, finding nothing but cubicles, dead computers, and jackets that had been left hanging on the backs of chairs. With each step, the banging got louder and louder. Eventually they followed it to a heavy door marked 'Physics Lab'.

Alexa brought the code up, typed it in, and pressed enter. Peanut and Ashan entered the room, weapons up and ready.

"About goddamn time you got here!" a severe-looking man in a lab coat exclaimed. "Do you have any idea how long we've been waiting?"

CHAPTER 10

"Step one, get out of the room," Teller commented.

"Your code worked one way, but not the other?" Monroe asked Janelle.

She nodded. "It got me in, but it sure as shit can't get me out."

De Vries examined the electronic keypad. Admittedly, to him it was just a mess of buttons. What he knew about technology was confined to the smartphone his grandson had gotten him for Christmas. But the keypad looked to be in working order.

"Try it again?" he suggested.

Janelle looked at him a moment, then back at Monroe, who nodded. She sighed, stepped forward, and keyed in her code. The keypad beeped once, twice, then the door slid open like they were in an episode of *Star Trek*.

"What the...?" Janelle said, stunned.

"We can question it later, my friend," De Vries said, "but for now, let's leave, hey?"

Outside was another sterile corridor. There were doors like the one they had just come through on each side, leading to various labs. De Vries noted the words on them, an involuntary shudder running down his back.

Jislaaik, what the fok have they been doing here? he thought to himself.

Monroe, who had taken point, held up his hand. The group stopped. The lieutenant pointed to a spot on the floor one door ahead of them. De Vries knew it was blood. Dark and discoloured, not fresh.

Another hand signal from Monroe, this time telling De Vries and Janelle to stay put. Both soldiers moved forward. They kept their steps light and silent on the hard floor.

Monroe hugged the wall next to the door. Teller stacked up behind him. At the count of three, both soldiers swept inward, Monroe taking left, Teller right.

Their brains processed the scene as only trained soldiers could, seeing and discounting irrelevant information. Blood, body, table, beakers. Everything happening in seconds. For De Vries, time had slowed, his heart in his throat. Janelle shifted nervously behind him.

"Contact!" Teller cried as something leapt at him.

He fired a burst from his rifle, the explosion deafening in the small space. The shots went wide as the thing barrelled into him, sending him sprawling backwards.

Monroe was already turning, finger tightening on the trigger as he acquired his target. But it was lightning fast. As soon as he saw it and fired, it was gone, out into the corridor.

De Vries was ready. He fired once, twice, three times, leading his target as it came into sight. The big .308 slugs flew straight and true. A geyser of dark red blood erupted on-target. The thing went down, twitching and emitting a savage growl.

Monroe and Teller were out seconds later, weapons ready. They needn't have bothered. The thing was dead, just a carcass leaking blood on the once-pristine floor. The smell of cordite and copper filled the team's nostrils.

"What is that?" Teller asked.

He stared at the thing in disbelief. De Vries did too, until he snapped out of it.

"That," he said, "is a bloody dinosaur."

CHAPTER 11

"Sir, I need you to stand back," Ashan said.

His weapon was at a 45-degree angle to the floor, ready to come up if the man in the lab coat in front of him did not back off. A woman stood behind and off to the left. She was doing her best to look non-threatening.

"You're here to save us, right?" the man demanded.

The man took a step forward and Ashan acted. He lowered his weapon and spun the man around, shoving him forward into the wall. His forearm was placed solidly in the man's back, pinning him there.

"Sir, I warned you," Ashan breathed.

"You son of a bitch!" the man yelled.

He was struggling now, doing his best to break free of the soldier. The woman was saying something, trying to keep him calm. Alexa stepped forward.

"Sir, stop moving!" she said.

Something in her voice made the man stop struggling. Even Ashan flinched. The woman had a voice that you listened to.

"Who are you?" Alexa asked.

She nodded to Ashan that it was safe. Ashan took two steps away from the man, but kept his rifle at the ready. If the aggressive bastard moved, he'd waste him.

"Doctor Waite," the man said, "and behind me is Lizzie."

"Doctor Elizabeth King. You can call me Lizzie. John, our lab tech, is hurt."

She motioned to a man lying in the corner of the room. He had a coat bundled up under his head. Peanut went to him.

Alexa pulled out her phone. She brought up pictures of the staff of the building and made sure that Waite and

Lizzie were who they said they were. With their identities confirmed, Ashan finally lowered his weapon.

"I'll have your…" Waite said, faltering on the word when he saw that Ashan wasn't a police officer. "I'll have whatever the equivalent of a badge is! I've never been treated like that in my life."

"Sir, he acted in accordance with SOP," Alexa said. "You were being aggressive. Now please keep quiet. Doctor King? Can you tell us what happened here?"

"I'm the senior scientist," Waite interjected.

"I'll get to you, sir. Doctor King?"

"Please, call me Lizzie," she said. "I… don't quite know what happened. We were running a test on our –"

"That's enough, Lizzie!" Waite said. "None of these people are cleared to know what we do here."

"Guys," Peanut said, standing, "I'm afraid he's gone."

Lizzie rushed over to him. She looked down at him. A sob escaped her lips.

"I'm sorry, ma'am," Peanut said awkwardly.

"I didn't even know him very well," she said.

Alexa put her hand on the young doctor's shoulder. "I am sorry, but we don't have time for this right now."

"She's right," Waite said, "we need to get to the basement. Unless I shut down the power to the entire building, Manhattan will cease to exist in a few hours."

***

"But I thought dinosaurs were like, scaley," Teller said, "like lizards."

The thing at their feet wasn't like any dinosaur Teller had seen at the movies with his kids. It was only about four feet tall, covered in blue feathers, with stubby arms that resembled wings, and a mess of feathers at the end of its tail. It had three claws on each wing and vicious-looking ones on its feet. A jaw full of razor-sharp teeth hung open in death.

"Their closest relatives are birds," De Vries said. "This one looks like a Troodon. Think mini raptor. Pretty smart too, from what I recall."

"So now you're an expert on dinosaurs too, man?"

De Vries laughed. "I have grandchildren, Teller. Boys, all of them. They love their dinosaur books at their age. Didn't you?"

"If you read more than princess books, Teller, you'd learn a thing or two," Monroe said with a smirk.

"No one going to freak out over the fact that we're fighting dinosaurs here?" Janelle asked.

"We just fell through two inter-dimensional portals in the space of fifteen minutes, Marine," Monroe said. "At this point, big lizards are the least surprising thing."

"Birds," De Vries said. "Big birds."

Monroe gave him a look. De Vries held up his hands in mock surrender.

"Alexa, Monroe here, we have updates."

"So do we. You first."

"We have hostiles in the form of..." Monroe looked at the dead dinosaur once again to remind himself that he wasn't going mad. "In the form of dinosaurs. I repeat. Dinosaurs."

"Copy that. We have another problem. We need to get to the basement to shut off auxiliary power to the building. If we don't, the equipment in this building is going to blow and take out most of Manhattan. We have four hours. Either we diffuse it, or we'll be too dead to worry anymore."

CHAPTER 12

"Did the L.T. just say *dinosaurs*?" Peanut asked in disbelief.

"It worked," Lizzie breathed, wonderment overcoming her grief for a moment. "My God, it actually worked."

"Lizzie," Waite warned.

"What worked, Doctor?" Alexa asked.

"We were trying to create a portal to somewhere else," Lizzie explained, ignoring Waite, "using that machine in there to generate portals to other dimensions! And we succeeded! I'm sorry, I know this situation is horrible, but this is incredible."

Alexa couldn't blame the doctor for being excited. Even she knew that this was a monumental discovery that would change the world of physics forever. But Alexa had a job to do and it involved saving lives.

"Lizzie, if you don't shut up, I'll have your job, girl!" Waite said. "None of these people are cleared and I will not have my life's work stolen by them."

"Blow it out your ass, Doctor Waite," Lizzie said.

Alexa smirked. "Calm down, both of you. You need to come with us. We have bigger worries than who gets the credit right now."

"Agreed," Waite said. "You have to get me to the basement. I'm the only one that knows how to safely shut down and restart the system. If I don't…"

"Okay then. Let's move. Lizzie, Doctor Waite, you obey any and all orders from us, no questions asked. Ashan, Peanut? Let's get moving. We've got a ton of floors between us and the basement."

"Yes, ma'am," Ashan said. "Lizzie, which way to the stairs?"

Lizzie pointed. The soldiers nodded, Ashan taking point, Alexa and the doctors staying close behind. Peanut and Ashan moved efficiently through the office, clearing corners as they went.

The fact that there was a credible threat that they had never faced before put them on edge. Their years in special operations had taught both soldiers how to deal with human insurgents. They knew their movements, their actions, how they operated. But dinosaurs? No damn training manual had ever covered that.

It took less than a minute to get to the stairs. They stacked up, opened the door, and swept the stairwell before motioning the rest to follow. Ashan noticed something on the next floor down. He held up his hand for the others, telling them to stop.

He took the stairs down sideways, doing his best to make no noise. A blood trail ran down from his level to the one below. Ashan followed it, his eyes going where his weapon aimed. It came into view slowly, like he was in a horror movie and the camera was panning round to give the audience a shock.

It was the body of a person. Whether man, woman, or otherwise, Ashan couldn't tell. Not anymore. They had been eviscerated, the walls coated in blood and gore. The smell of rot and the bacteria from the intestines made Ashan gag. He took a breath through his mouth.

"Clear!" he called up to the others. "But prepare yourselves. It ain't pretty down here."

Ashan moved in front of the body, doing his best to block it from the two civilians as much as possible. He didn't want their morale taking too bad a hit this early on in the mission.

Peanut let out a whistle on seeing the corpse. He shook his head, but said nothing. He'd seen worse. Admittedly only in the aftermath of suicide bombs and IEDs. The thought that something living and breathing could have done this made him shudder. He was just about to start down to the next floor when something snarled.

Ashan heard it too. He motioned to Alexa, who nodded, pushing the doctors behind her. Peanut stopped moving. He listened. A clicking sound reached his ears, like the sound of his dog's claws on the tiles when he ran about the house.

Which could only mean one thing.

Ashan tapped Peanut on the back, letting him know that he was ready. The two men started downwards, Peanut on point. The clicking continued, claws scraping against the tiled floor of the stairwell. Another growl, this one closer.

Peanut's muscles tensed involuntarily, but he kept moving. Step by step. Quiet and smooth, as his training and operations experience had drilled into him.

The building started to shake. A low rumble at first but it wasn't long until it was violent enough to rattle Peanut's internal organs. He lost his footing, his boot slipping on the smooth step, the rumble throwing him further off balance so that he couldn't correct himself.

Peanut fell, sailing down one flight of steps and hitting the next landing with a jolt that rattled his brain around his skull. Then he saw them. Dinosaurs, blue feathered things with vicious fangs and inhuman eyes that locked onto him. He knew the look. He was prey.

Around him the walls were shaking. Ashan steadied himself on the railing while trying to make it to his comrade. Waite was yelling about something, but neither soldier could make out what it was.

Peanut felt the hairs on his arms stand as the air crackled with energy once more. Another portal was opening somewhere nearby.

The creatures, which were nothing like any dinosaurs Peanut had ever seen in the movies, were coming towards him now. They snarled and called, their unfamiliar environment making them hostile.

Peanut didn't think, he just fired. He was lying on his side, weapon aimed at an odd angle. The shots went wide, shattering the concrete wall just above the heads of the dinosaurs. Chips of stone and dust rained down on them, startling them both.

One of the dinosaurs had had enough. It lunged, using its powerful legs to leap up towards Peanut. He struggled to get his weapon on target, the odd angle he was lying in and the constant shaking making it damn near impossible to do so.

Ashan called a warning from above as the thing landed a few steps down and leapt again. He'd slung his rifle and drawn his pistol as he held on tight to the railing. He fired now, letting off shots in rapid succession, the semi-automatic doing its thing.

With everything that was happening, Ashan knew that there was no way that his shots would land. He was just hoping that they spooked the creature somehow. Threw it off course. It sailed through the air like a living rocket, its second jump somehow more powerful than the first.

Peanut saw the thing coming towards him, all teeth and claws and rage. He braced himself for impact, knowing that the creature's fellow was right behind it. He could hear its claws scrabbling for purchase on the floor.

There was a sudden burst of static. Blue rained down onto Peanut. The smell of burnt ozone mingled with the stench of gunpowder and death in the air.

Finally, the shaking stopped. In front of Peanut lay a dinosaur's severed leg, the portal having closed around the poor thing before it was all the way through. It twitched and jumped and smoked as it bled. The stink of charred flesh filled the air. He kicked it down the stairs.

"You okay, man?" Ashan asked, finally able to reach his friend.

49

Ashan scanned for any threats, seeing none. But he could hear claws on tiles as the other dinosaur fled down the stairs. Peanut sat up with his back against the wall. He took a breath, reloaded his rifle, and stood with a smile plastered across his face.

"Bro, that was a fucking trip," he breathed.

CHAPTER 13

Monroe breathed a sigh of relief as the shaking finally subsided. He wondered whether the building could take it or if it would just crumble underneath their feet during one of the quakes. Not only that, but the electrical fluctuations caused by the temporal disturbances were playing hell with their radios.

"You have any idea what they were doing in these labs, Marine?" the lieutenant asked.

Janelle shrugged. "Most of us operate on a strictly need to know basis, sir. Even the scientists have their work compartmentalised."

"Any bioweapons?"

"I suspect so. They pay us too well not to be guarding something important. Most of the security are ex-military."

"So, where are they?" De Vries asked. "I know you Americans have a good military, hey? A couple of dinosaurs couldn't have taken out your entire security team."

"It's been radio silence for hours now, sir."

"Can you get us to the basement?" Teller asked.

Janelle nodded. "Yes sir, I can. We need to take the stairs though. Elevators were the first to shut down."

"I'm cool with stairs, man. I think I've had enough of elevators for a while."

Monroe's radio crackled. The words were heavily distorted with static.

"… coming… towards… hostiles…"

"This is Monroe. Repeat your last, over."

The reply was just as garbled. Monroe cursed.

"Something about hostiles," he said to the others. "Keep your eyes and ears open."

The group nodded. De Vries felt like he was in a dream, what with the sheer amount of crazy shit happening around him. What else could be waiting for them at the lower levels?

A rustling sound behind them stopped De Vries in his tracks. He looked back down the corridor. There it was again, like paper blowing in the wind. Lots of it. He tapped Monroe on the shoulder, pointing down.

Monroe looked, holding up a hand to stop the team. It was getting louder. A door at the end of the hall burst open and a flying mass spewed out from it.

The sound of leathery wings flapping combined with the screeches of the animals as they surged down the corridor towards Monroe, De Vries, and the others. All they could see was wings and eyes and teeth all jumbled up in a rolling wave that was heading straight for them.

"Run!" De Vries called, already turning.

No one needed to be told twice. They ran, the mass of flying creatures gaining on them as they sprinted away. De Vries could feel the air from the sheer number of them tickling his neck as he ran. His leg was protesting, but he ignored it, trying his best to concentrate on running faster.

Something latched onto his back. A searing pain shot through his body as the creature dug deep into his flesh. He let out a surprised cry of pain, stumbling as he ran.

Monroe scooped him up before he could fall and pushed him onwards. Ahead, Janelle turned and fired off a few rounds with her pistol. The bullets made the same difference to the mass as if she had spat on them.

The screeching of the creatures intensified. The corridor amplified the sound, filling their ears until they could hear nothing else. Their minds rebelled at the sheer overload being forced upon their senses.

De Vries reached back, ripping the thing off of his back. A fresh wave of pain swept over him as the creature took chunks of his flesh with it. He hurled the feathered thing back towards its brethren in disgust.

"I've got an idea!" Teller yelled.

He started to drop back, urging the others to keep going. He yanked a flashbang grenade from his belt, pulled the pin, and flung it into the seething mass of feathers and teeth, barely breaking stride as he did so.

"Flash out!" Teller called.

The grenade detonated with an almost impossibly loud concussive blast that was even heard over the noise of the animals themselves. A blinding white flash filled the corridor from within the mass.

Their cries were intensified by shock and pain, the group stopping and splintering into smaller ones. Some fell to the floor dead. Others reversed course.

Janelle was the first one to reach the stairwell door. She hit it shoulder first, barrelling into it at considerable speed. It flew inwards, smashing against the wall behind it with a loud bang.

Monroe was seconds behind her, then De Vries, who practically fell through the doorway. The only reason he didn't fall over was because he managed to lean into the wall. Teller was through last, yelling at Janelle to close the door, which she did. She slammed it shut with such force that the doorframe rocked.

Monroe and Janelle braced themselves against it swiftly after, breathing hard and waiting. It wasn't long before the door shuddered, opening a crack as the mass of flying predators slammed into it. But the two managed to close it again, Janelle flipping the lock just in time.

"Jesus," Teller breathed. "You okay, brother?"

De Vries was leaning against the wall, sucking in air like a broken vacuum. His heart rate was going crazy, his back was on fire, and his leg was struggling to be heard over all the other pain. He nodded anyway.

"Fine, my China," he replied, "just old."

Teller laughed. "You're never too old, unless you're dead. Now let me take a look at that wound."

"How bad is it?" De Vries asked as he turned around.

Teller examined the wound. Blood had already started to soak through the uniform that De Vries was wearing. A jagged tear, about an inch and a half long, was visible in his body armour.

"Brother, whatever those things were, one of them ripped straight through your body armour back here," Teller said. "Otherwise, it's not that bad. Get your armour and shirt off, I'll patch you up."

"Marine, watch nothing comes down on us," Monroe said. "I'll make sure nothing comes up."

De Vries stripped to the waist, allowing Teller to disinfect the wound before applying a field dressing. De Vries winced as the disinfectant did its work. The door continued to rattle as the creatures slammed into it.

"All done," Teller said. "Want something for the pain?"

De Vries shook his head. "I'm used to it."

"Good to go?" Monroe asked.

Everyone nodded.

"Down we go then."

"I wonder what else we're going to run into," Teller whispered to himself.

CHAPTER 14

"Radio's fucked," Alexa declared.

"Lovely," Peanut commented.

Lizzie was examining the dinosaur leg on the floor. Waite looked disinterested. Ashan couldn't help but wonder why, since he'd have thought the doctor would be thrilled with the results of his experiment.

"Come on, Doc," Alexa said. "Four hours, remember?"

"Of course," Lizzie said, standing, "it's just fascinating! We have genuine, living dinosaurs roaming around an office building in Manhattan. Do you realise what this means?"

"Yeah," Peanut said, "a massive fucking cleaning bill. How much do dinosaurs shit anyway?"

Lizzie gave him her best unimpressed look. He chuckled, holding up his hands in mock surrender.

"It's really great and all, Doc," Ashan said, "but can we celebrate *after* we disarm the bomb?"

"He's right," Waite said. "Come on. We must move."

Alexa grabbed his arm. "Let the soldiers go first, Doctor Waite."

He rolled his eyes, but stood back to let Ashan and Peanut pass. Ashan just barely managed to hold his tongue to stop from cursing out the old bastard. He was used to people like Waite, having grown up Muslim in the United States.

"Um, guys," Peanut said, "we got a problem."

Ashan joined him on the landing to the next floor. He let out a low whistle. Vines, thick, green, and gnarled, had grown through the walls and blocked the stairwell. Ashan reached out, brushing his fingers across the flesh of the thing to make sure he wasn't seeing things.

"Fascinating," Lizzie said, running up to examine the vegetation. "They seem to have smashed straight through the walls. Do you think this is happening throughout the building, Doctor Waite?"

"Quite possibly," Waite said. "This is a tad inconvenient for us, however."

"Can you cut through?" Alexa asked.

Peanut shook his head. "Too thick for our knives. We could maybe blast through, but without knowing how thick this shit is, I wouldn't advise it."

Ashan pushed open the door next to him. It took some effort to do so, and when he'd finally forced it open, he discovered why. His jaw dropped. Behind the door was a jungle, one that had grown inside the building.

"How in the hell?" he breathed.

Vegetation was everywhere: the floor, the walls, growing through windows. Vines snaked about, in some cases going through the walls. A few trees were dotted about, one having grown in from one level down. Bugs crawled through the undergrowth. A snake lounged on a branch. Animal sounds could be heard coming from within the foliage.

Lizzie was at a loss for words. She just stared, half fascinated and half curious. Her scientific mind was trying – and failing – to figure out how all of this could have happened.

"Perhaps the portals let growth through and somehow accelerated it?" Waite wondered aloud.

"If I'd known I was gonna be exploring a jungle, I'd have brought my machete," Peanut said.

Alexa was tapping away on her phone again. She was scrolling through maps, doing her best to figure out a way to get to the lower levels.

"Looks like we have no choice, guys," she said at last. "We have to go through it."

***

A few floors down, Monroe, De Vries, and the others had run into their own problem. They'd found the second dinosaur from earlier, but that wasn't the issue. The poor thing was already dead. It had raced down the stairs only to find that three entire flights were completely missing and fallen to its death.

"This is a whack ass day, brother," Teller said.

It looked as if someone had reached in and ripped the stairs out of the building. Loose bricks, mortar, and bits of rebar hung at odd angles. As they watched, a piece of concrete fell and smashed itself to dust three floors down.

"Elevator it is," Monroe said.

"Looks like it," De Vries said.

He winced as they turned back towards the door into the next floor. The good thing about having his back nearly shredded was that it took away some of the pain of his leg. It had been a long time since it had taken such a beating.

Monroe and Teller stacked up, nodded, then went through the door. It was another long corridor with labs on either side of it.

"If I'm not mistaken, this is one of the bio lab floors," Janelle said.

"Possible contamination?" Monroe asked.

She shook her head. "We'd know."

"How?" De Vries asked.

"The doors would seal, an alarm would sound, and we'd most likely be dead."

"Sounds *lekker.*"

"Where are all the other people?" Teller asked.

"I don't know, sir," Janelle replied. "We should have run into more by now. This building has hundreds working in it. Not just scientists. Security, office staff, janitors."

"What's the SOP for emergencies?" Monroe said as they started down the corridor.

"Security clears each floor. We take everyone down to a holding area on the first floor, which is basically a huge event room. Head count done there. Then we sit tight and wait for further orders. But comms went down so fast, I have no idea if any of that happened."

"Would the civvies sit tight to wait for security?"

Janelle nodded.

De Vries was about to say something when an animal call echoed down the hall towards them. Everyone stopped dead in their tracks. In seconds, there were four weapons aimed towards the source of the sound.

"That sounded like–" Teller started.

"A raptor," De Vries finished.

CHAPTER 15

The jungle around them had somehow brought its atmosphere with it. The heat was stifling, the humidity so cloying that clothes stuck uncomfortably to flesh. Every breath felt difficult, like they were breathing soup, not air.

It was a struggle to move, the foliage was so dense. Ashan had to force his way through, parting leaves and branches before holding it back to let the others through. A cacophony of noise assaulted their ears. Insects buzzed, animals called, and things screeched. Everyone was on-edge, even Ashan and Peanut.

There was no telling what lurked in the forest around them.

"Hard to tell where we're going in this mess," Ashan said.

"We're heading in the right direction," Alexa said. "Just keep straight if you can."

Something ahead caught Ashan's eye. He stopped, peering into the undergrowth. Movement. Subtle, but it was there. He could see a pattern gliding through the bush.

Ashan told the others to stop before he crept forward. He needed to get closer to see what it was. The pattern was familiar. Scales that shone in the somehow still functioning artificial light from the bulbs overhead.

"Fuck," he breathed, realisation dawning at last.

It was part of a snake, slithering through the jungle. A massive snake. The section of the creature that was visible was at least twice as big as his thigh and it just kept gliding past. Desperately, he searched for the head of the reptile as he backed up.

Alexa saw Ashan start his retreat. She motioned to Peanut to let him know that there was danger ahead and pushed the doctors against the wall. She couldn't see what Ashan was backing away from. Her mind raced with possibilities, her muscles tensing and grip tightening on her pistol.

Ashan was two steps away from Alexa and the doctors when the wall behind him exploded in a shower of plaster dust and fragments of vegetation. Doctor Waite screamed a high-pitched yell of sheer terror as an enormous snake's head hissed at them from the opening it had just created.

The debris from the wall knocked Alexa forwards. The breath was forced out of her lungs as she flew into a tangle of vines. Lizzie was already moving, diving away from the snake, yelling at the others to shoot it.

Despite the horror and absurdity of the situation, Ashan's training took over. He raised his weapon and tried to take aim at the thing's head, which was at least twice as big as a man's. But Waite, who was still screaming, was in the way.

Peanut responded as well, spinning around and taking aim. He let loose a volley of shots into the wall around the snake's head, unable to get a clear shot with Waite in the way, but trying his best to scare the creature.

A piece of concrete hit the thing in its right eye. It thrashed violently from side to side, hissing in pain. The head connected with Waite, sending him sailing into Ashan. The two men landed on the snake's enormous body, which immediately started to coil around them.

The snake's head disappeared through the hole, causing Peanut's next burst of shots to shred drywall. Lizzie was already scrambling to her feet to get to Alexa and help her up. The agent was tangled up in the vines and couldn't free herself.

"Peanut! Knife!" Lizzie called, rushing to Alexa's aid.

Peanut drew and tossed his combat knife, one-handed. Lizzie caught it, setting to work hacking at the greenery that had wrapped itself around Alexa.

Waite scrabbled away from the snake's body before it could close around him, his hands clawing at the undergrowth as he dragged himself forward. Ashan was too winded to move fast. He could feel the scaly, muscular body begin to wrap itself around his. His arms were pinned to his sides and he was unable to use his weapons.

Peanut charged forward as the snake's head appeared out of a doorway, knowing that it had prey to constrict. He fired from the hip, sending a volley of 5.56mm NATO rounds into the reptile's flesh. It hissed in agony and began to thrash once more, dark blood splashing everywhere.

As soon as Lizzie had finally chopped her way through the last vine that clung to Alexa, the agent leapt to her feet, scooping up her weapon as she did so. Waite had gotten onto his hands and knees by then and was still crawling away from the snake.

More explosions thundered in the enclosed space as Peanut emptied the rest of his magazine into the snake. Ashan was already finding it hard to breathe, the snake having already wrapped itself entirely around him. With each breath he let out, the animal coiled itself tighter.

Alexa took in the situation in a fraction of a second. She raced forwards with her pistol, heading straight for the reptile's head. Peanut was reloading, ejecting his spent magazine and slapping a fresh one home in less than a second. But Alexa was on the thing before he could fire again.

She jammed her Sig under the snake's jaw and pulled the trigger again and again. A fountain of gore followed, showering over her and the surrounding vegetation, turning it red and slick with blood and brain matter.

At last, the snake collapsed dead. Alexa's barrage of bullets had removed its head from its body, leaving nothing but a bloody stump.

Peanut and Alexa were already helping Ashan, wrenching and pulling and yanking at the dead reptile's strong body. Sweat coated them in seconds and they did their best to control the death throes of the animal. Lizzie grabbed the tail end and unwrapped it as quickly as she could.

As the snake came away from his chest, Ashan let out a gasp. He collapsed to the floor, gulping in as much air as possible, a stab of pain following every gulp as his bruised ribs screamed in protest.

"Is he okay?" Alexa asked.

Ashan held up a shaky hand and gave her a thumbs up. Lizzie rolled him over to check him out.

"Jesus Christ," Peanut said, looking up at Alexa.

Her face was coated with blood and pieces of snake flesh. She looked like a demon that had just crawled its way up from hell. Peanut pulled a cloth out of his pocket and handed it to her.

"That snake did not know who it was fucking with," he said.

CHAPTER 16

"Great, now we're in a Spielberg movie," Teller said. "This day is going just peachy so far."

More raptor calls came from up ahead. The group kept dead still, their weapons all aimed down the corridor. They could hear the creatures moving about as their claws ticked and scraped on the floor.

"De Vries," Monroe whispered, "what do we do?"

De Vries considered their options. There was only one. The elevator lobby was halfway along the corridor on the right. They'd just have to hope that the dinosaurs were further along.

"We move," De Vries hissed, "slow and steady."

Monroe and De Vries took the lead, Teller and Janelle right behind them. They walked carefully, rolling their feet with each step, doing their best to reduce the noise they were making. Each of them was fighting to keep their breathing steady; to control the adrenaline rush and fear that was creeping into their hearts.

It was an agonisingly slow walk. Each step seemed to take forever, like they were all moving in slow motion. De Vries kept his eyes peeled, ready to fire at the first sign of danger. None of them were expecting the floor to disappear from underneath their feet.

The fall was mercifully short this time, ensuring that all of them landed on their feet. They found themselves surrounded by jungle terrain. Huge, towering trees, thick undergrowth, and a ground covered in gnarled roots, dead foliage, and small plants. And all around them were the calls of raptors.

"What the fuck just happened?" Janelle asked, spinning around.

"Eyes open," Monroe ordered, "we've got hostiles in the trees."

Something lunged out of the undergrowth towards Janelle. All she saw was teeth and claws flying towards her, spittle dripping from dangerous jaws.

De Vries grabbed her by the collar, yanking her backwards as the raptor sailed past. Teller spun and opened fire as the creature crashed into the undergrowth. A volley of bullets was followed closely by an inhuman cry of pain.

Monroe saw another one of the dinosaurs, feathers covering its body, intelligent eyes, and vicious sharp teeth and claws. It opened its mouth to roar before charging forward towards the group. He put it down with a burst of automatic fire to the thing's head, spreading blood and brain matter across the leaves behind it.

The call to charge given, more raptors burst forth from the jungle. Everyone started shooting, picking their shots as carefully as they could in the chaos. The air was filled with the smell of gunpowder and burnt flesh.

Roars and screams of anger and pain assaulted their ears even as the air around them was filled with raw energy once more. The group found themselves weightless for a split second before the ground met them. Teller screamed in pain as he landed on his leg, snapping his tibia clean in half.

The raptors were just as surprised as the humans to find themselves in an unfamiliar environment. Now, surrounded by harsh artificial light, their claws barely finding purchase on the smooth, sterile floor, their anger and bewilderment made them even more aggressive.

One of the creatures managed to clamp its jaws onto Janelle's left forearm as she was reloading. Razor-sharp teeth cut through her flesh as if it were butter, piercing straight to the bone. Janelle yelled in pain and anger and began to batter the thing over the top of the head with her pistol.

Monroe dragged Teller behind him as he was firing at the raptors. Jaws snapped closed perilously close to him as they tried to get at their prey. His magazine clicked empty as another made a leap for him.

The lieutenant dropped his rifle and drew his pistol in less than a second, barely having time to get the weapon up as the raptor was coming towards him. He was pulling the trigger even as the thing crashed into him, sending both of them tumbling backwards.

"You motherfucker!" Janelle yelled, cracking the creature's skull with the butt of her weapon.

The thing screamed, its jaws finally releasing. It stumbled backwards, dazed, and De Vries shot it in the head, using the last round in his magazine. He ejected the spent mag, slapping a fresh one home and bringing his rifle up to resume firing.

But he found no targets. The hallway was littered with the bodies of dead and dying creatures. It was over.

"Monroe," De Vries called.

Monroe was trying to get the body of the dead raptor off of him. His pistol rounds had found their target, shredding the thing's heart even as it had landed on top of him. De Vries dragged the heavy body off of the lieutenant to reveal a blood-soaked man underneath.

He helped Monroe to his feet before attending to Janelle's shredded, bloodied arm. Monroe crouched next to Teller to examine the man's leg. It was bent at an odd angle below the knee. It looked unnatural and sickening.

"It's fucked, sir," Teller said through gritted teeth.

De Vries helped Janelle sit down next to Teller. Her forearm looked as if a madman had attacked it with a steak knife.

"Teller, field dressing and bandages?" De Vries asked.

Teller fished them out of his pouch. He handed them over and De Vries set to work. Janelle screamed an obscenity as he poured disinfectant over the wound.

"You gonna warn me next time?" she hissed.

De Vries apologised as he proceeded to wrap her arm up. He made sure that it was tight in order to stop the bleeding.

"You need to splint the leg," Teller was saying to Monroe. "Set it and splint it."

"Looks like it," Monroe agreed. "Ready?"

Teller nodded. Monroe took hold of the leg, counted to three, then snapped it back into place. Teller squirmed against the wall, as if he were trying to climb it to get away from the pain. Bile rose in his throat that he barely managed to keep down. Tears formed in his eyes.

"Now we just need something to act as a splint."

CHAPTER 17

Fortune smiled on them, for as Alexa and the group were making their way to the elevator shaft, they came upon a massive tree. The thing had somehow taken root three floors down and had forced its way to their level with surprising effectiveness.

Waite made a comment about accelerated growth, but since he had failed to carry himself admirably during the fight with the snake, everyone ignored him. It was Lizzie that suggested they climb down the mighty, gnarled trunk. Since everyone was tired of having their nerves rattled by the thick jungle around them, they agreed.

Peanut was the last one to step off the trunk. He was thankful that their new environment was less densely populated with plants than the thicket above. He'd never thought he'd be happy to see the harsh glare of artificial light before.

"We not gonna talk about what we just saw?" Peanut said.

Ashan shook his head. "It's dead. We have to keep moving forward."

"But that was the biggest fucking snake I've ever seen!"

"Titanoboa," Lizzie said, "about 60 million years old."

"It looked pretty lively to me. These are definitely time portals, then?"

"Maybe. Or they could be portals to other dimensions, where life took different paths than it did in ours."

"Does it really matter?" Alexa asked. "I mean, right now our most pressing issue is getting to the basement. We learn what we can along the way, Doc, but anything that doesn't help our situation can wait."

"I agree," Lizzie replied, "I'm just finding all of this so damn interesting. I can't help it."

"Nice to be doing something you enjoy," Peanut commented, "like fleeing 60-million-year-old reptiles."

"What else is there to do? Scream and cry? Fuck that. This is our greatest scientific achievement ever and if I die, I want to die happy."

"For once, we agree wholeheartedly, Lizzie," Waite said. "Although I'd prefer to live."

They kept moving, the foliage thinning out to nothing as they got closer to the stairwell door. Alexa pushed it open slowly, revealing impenetrable darkness beyond.

"Something's wrong," Waite said. "The emergency power should be powering lights in the stairwell."

"I'll take point," Ashan said. "Peanut, watch our six. Flashlights on. Everyone move slow and steady. Watch your footing."

The two soldiers clicked on the flashlights attached to their rifles. Ashan stepped through the doorway and into the darkness. His light cut a path through it, revealing the stairs leading down.

Ashan started moving, taking each step slowly and cautiously. Alexa kept close, followed by Waite, Lizzie, and Peanut. Ashan couldn't shake the feeling that something was watching him, peering at him from out of the black. The hairs on the back of his neck stood on end.

"Keep alert," he whispered to Alexa, who passed the message down.

There was nothing on the next landing, or the one below that. Yet that feeling of being watched by ravenous eyes wasn't going away. Ashan glanced about as he descended, his heart thumping in his chest. The little voice in his head, the same one that had kept him alive on countless missions, was yelling at him, screaming danger.

But where?

Then he heard it. A rustling, like leaves in the breeze. A chill ran down his spine. It was louder now, emanating from the gloom around them. No, not around. *Above.*

Slowly, Ashan aimed his weapon upwards. His breath caught in his throat when the light caught on thousands of beady black eyes. They stared at him for a brief moment, confused at being caught in the glare of the flashlight. Then, as if in slow motion, hundreds of tiny mouths filled with razor-sharp teeth opened and screamed as one.

They're covering the ceiling lights!

The thought popped into Ashan's head as the things took off. The stairwell became filled with beating wings, animal screeching, and small flying bodies.

"Run!" Ashan shouted.

They ran, forcing their way through the seething mass of creatures around them. They crushed so close that Alexa was struggling to breathe. Sharp claws ripped at the skin of her cheek. She felt blood flow.

Ashan was using his rifle as a club, waving it back and forth to try and clear a path. Behind him, Peanut opened fire. The creatures screamed louder, getting even more frenzied than before. One of them landed in Lizzie's hair and she ripped it off, throwing it back into the crowd of things around them.

It felt like they were swimming through thick, unyielding sludge. The thing flew and screeched and scratched and bit. Ashan kept fighting towards the door on the floor below, clubbing this way and that. Some of the creatures fell to the floor, stunned.

Alexa was dragging Lizzie and Waite downwards, their hands clamped firmly in both of hers. She'd holstered her weapon soon after the creatures had taken flight, knowing that it would be useless against so many of the things.

Ashan got to the door at last. He slung his weapon and wrenched the door open. He had to strain against the living mass around him. They seemed to be actively forcing the door closed.

It took less than twenty seconds for Alexa to arrive by his side and grab hold. Together they managed to pull the door open all the way. Waite went through first, followed by Lizzie. Alexa was pushed through by Ashan. The special agent practically fell into the corridor beyond, sprawling forwards onto the floor.

Peanut dove through, grabbing Ashan's vest as he did so, pulling his friend with him. The door slammed shut almost immediately. A few of the creatures that had made it into the corridor screamed and flew off. The door thumped behind them as the mass slammed against it.

"Fuck me," Peanut breathed, "I guess we ain't getting downstairs that way."

CHAPTER 18

"There should be a first aid kit in the room at the end of the hall," Janelle said, pointing.

"Okay," Monroe nodded. "Janelle, you stay here with Teller. De Vries, with me."

De Vries and Monroe hurried down to the other end of the corridor. The lieutenant opened the door slowly, going in weapon first. He found what looked like a recreation room with a fridge, a kitchenette. and a couple of chairs. Mounted on the wall was a first aid station.

De Vries went straight to the chairs. They were cheap things, no more than plastic seats set onto metal legs. He leaned his weapon against the wall and proceeded to rip two of the legs off one of the chairs. The thin metal gave easily.

"Got your friend a splint," he said, holding them up.

"Good. I got us some bandages here."

Monroe had finished going through the first aid box. He'd taken everything of use. They headed back to Teller. His face was coated in a fine sheen of sweat.

De Vries held the two bits of chair leg in place while Monroe wrapped a bandage around them. He wrapped it tight, each turn causing Teller to flinch in pain. Once he was done, he tied it off.

Janelle helped the wounded man up. Teller leaned against her as he stood, using her as a makeshift crutch. Another wince passed his face as he tested his leg.

"Good to go, LT," he said, although he didn't look it.

"Good man," Monroe said.

He tried his radio and got nothing but static in return.

"I guess we assume that our friends aren't going to make it," De Vries said.

"Safe assumption," Monroe commented. "But yes, you're right. We need to get to the basement. Janelle, is there anywhere that you and Teller can hole up?"

Janelle thought for a moment. "Two floors down there's a security station. Two doors in, both reinforced steel. Might be weapons in there too. We could bunker down in there."

"Sounds like a plan. You good to suffer through a couple of flights of stairs, Mike?"

Teller grinned. "As long as you don't expect me to take them two at a time."

De Vries and Monroe took point, heading towards the stairwell. There was still a thick blanket of tension in the air that had De Vries on edge. It felt like there was danger nearby, but he couldn't put his finger on where it was.

They reached the stairwell. Monroe took up position beside it, then nodded to De Vries. The lieutenant pushed the door open to let the older man sweep and clear.

Inside was clear, but De Vries could hear the leathery rustling of wings above his head. He looked up between the stairs. All he could see was a black mass about two floors up. A shudder ran through him. The flying things from earlier on.

He turned to the rest, held a finger to his lips, then pointed upwards. Everyone else nodded. The message was crystal clear. Keep quiet and move down as fast as they could.

Monroe whispered that he'd protect their six. De Vries nodded and waited for the okay from Janelle and Teller before he started down.

Janelle's time in the Marines had made her fit. Since she'd left, she had hit the weights even harder. Teller could feel her muscles, as strong as steel beneath her clothes. Teller wondered if the woman was stronger than he was. He figured it was entirely possible, especially considering how easily she took his weight.

But even with her help, each step was pure agony. Teller was a SEAL, so he wasn't going to admit how much pain he was in until he couldn't bear it. He simply gritted his teeth against the pain. Hard.

Janelle noticed the tears in her partner's eyes. She adjusted her hold on him, making sure that she took most of the weight. Even with her strength, she was starting to sweat. Anyone would if they were supporting a full-grown man and his combat kit.

Up above, the rustling of wings continued. One or two of the creatures screeched. Janelle forced herself not to look up, even though her mind was filled with visions of the things descending upon her and stripping the flesh from her bones in seconds.

Two steps up and Monroe was having the same thoughts. His neck itched. It felt like thousands of tiny black eyes were fixed on him, just waiting for the right time to pounce. What made it worse was how slow progress was.

It had taken almost three minutes to get down one flight of stairs. On the last step, Teller's good leg almost slipped. Only quick thinking by Janelle had stopped him falling on his ass. He bit down hard on his lip to stop from screaming as his bad leg was jolted against the floor.

Once the wave of agony had passed, he nodded his thanks to Janelle. She gave him a small, reassuring smile in return.

De Vries went down to the next landing only after Teller had conquered a flight. There were three more flights to go now. Below them, everything looked clear. He couldn't hear anything either.

Up above was a different story. The creatures had become anxious for some reason. He could hear them darting about and screeching. Perhaps they sensed prey.

Teller managed to keep his leg from being jolted as they stepped onto the next landing. He heard Janelle let out a soft sigh of relief. Just two more flights to go. He could feel his heart pumping in his chest, but it wasn't just because of the pain. Those flying things were growing restless.

Monroe was about to follow down the stairs when razor-sharp claws hooked themselves in the back of his neck. He let out an involuntary yell of pain as warm blood began to roll down his back. The creature shrieked in satisfaction, its call soon joined by thousands of others.

Teller looked up at the cries from above him. He cursed a blue streak.

"Janelle, we need to pick up the pace!" he cried.

De Vries pushed past the two of them, running up to help Monroe out, who was still struggling to get the creature off the back of his neck. It scratched and clawed at him, shredding his skin as if it were paper.

De Vries used the butt of his rifle to smack the thing in the head. It died instantly as its skull was crushed by the impact, finally relaxing its grip and falling to the floor.

Monroe didn't waste time on apologies. He swung around and opened fire on the mass as it came towards them. Some of the creatures dropped as the bullets tore through their bodies. As he fired, he felt hands patting him down.

"Now is not the time for a romantic moment!" Monroe called.

"I'm looking for..." De Vries grinned suddenly, "...THIS!"

As the screeching grew louder, De Vries popped the prized. It was a signal flare. Suddenly, the stairwell was bathed in a harsh red light. Smoke drifted upwards towards the ceiling.

De Vries threw it towards the creatures. It had the desired effect. The seething mass of bodies swerved away from the harsh glare of the flare. Some let out screeches of annoyance that scratched at Monroe's ears.

"Run!" De Vries said, grabbing the lieutenant by the shoulder and shoving him down the stairs.

It wasn't long before they caught up with Janelle and Teller, who were on the last flight. Seeing them, Teller pushed Janelle away from him and dove down the rest of the way. He hit the floor with a thump, letting out a scream of pain as the impact jolted his broken leg once more. His vision swam, spots appearing before his eyes as the agony took over all of his senses.

Monroe rushed past him and yanked the door open. Janelle and De Vries grabbed Teller. They ran towards the open door, dragging the injured man with them. He was still crying out in pain as Monroe slammed the door shut behind them.

De Vries let go of Teller as soon as they were safe, bringing his rifle up to scan the room ahead. What he saw was so surprising that all he could do was stand with his mouth agape at the spectacle before him.

CHAPTER 19

"Sweet mother of God," Peanut breathed.

The floor they were on was a complete mess. Shell casings littered the floor. Blood was smeared across the walls. Bodies and pieces of bodies were scattered about.

"I smell smoke," Alexa said.

"And worse," Peanut said. "Are we in hell? I mean, seriously guys, are we in hell?"

Ashan helped him to his feet. "If this were hell, we'd know, brother."

"You sure about that? 'Cause I feel like we're in hell."

"Cut the damn chatter," Alexa hissed, "I hear something."

The two soldiers brought their rifles up. It wasn't just a sterile white corridor in front of them. The floor was divided into two halves. The part that they were in was full of furniture and plants, and looked to be a waiting or rest area. A wall blocked the other half from view, the doors leading into it standing open.

Alexa strained her ears. She'd heard something in the room, she was sure of it. But she couldn't be sure what it was. She pushed Lizzie and Waite behind her with her free hand, taking a step forward as she did so.

From somewhere in the room, something growled. A low, menacing sound. It almost sounded like a warning.

Everyone with a weapon had it aimed in the direction of the sound. The two soldiers steadied their breathing as they searched for the threat. Whatever it was, it sounded big.

A sudden scraping sound brought Alexa's eyes to the doors at the other end of the room. The darkness within made it impossible to see what had made it. Something growled again, the sound coming from elsewhere this time.

"Fuck me," she breathed.

More than one...

One of the doors creaked open slowly as something pushed its way through. Alexa's breath caught in her throat at the sight, as a massive dinosaur with a feathered ridge on its head stepped out into the light.

Small, feathered arms ended in razor-sharp claws. A mouth full of teeth snarled at them. And as it stepped forward, the cause of the scraping was revealed to be the vicious 12-inch-long claws on the creature's hind legs.

"Utahraptor," Alexa heard Waite say behind her.

Everyone stood stock still as the creature finally stopped moving. It sniffed the air with its snout. Drool dripped steadily from one side of its mouth. Alexa watched in horror as the thing turned its gaze towards the group.

A low growl from their left heralded the appearance of another of the massive creatures as it pushed aside a two-seater couch with a horrific scraping sound. Yet another popped its head out from behind a plant on the right. Three pairs of eyes turned towards the group, glinting dully in the emergency lighting.

For a moment, everything stopped. Dinosaurs and humans eyed each other quietly, each deciding their next move. Drool hit the floor with a wet splash. Alexa noticed blood coating the mouth of the Utahraptor on the left.

Slowly, inch by inch, Alexa raised her weapon, taking aim at the dinosaur directly in front of them. She had no idea whether her rounds would even make a difference to the massive creature, but what other choice did she have? There was no going back the way they had come.

Time stood still. Hearts pounded in chests. Blood raged and rushed loud in the ears of the people.

The first raptor moved.

Alexa's brain didn't even register the movement. She just acted on instinct, pulling the trigger as fast as she could as the massive creature leapt towards the group with an almighty roar.

The dinosaur's cry seemed to be the signal because the others leapt as well. The room was suddenly filled with the heat of muzzle flash and the deafening explosion of gunfire.

Alexa's first two rounds clipped the Utahraptor in the head. They scraped against the skull and ricocheted off into the wall behind the creature. Several feathers fell from the thing's head as it howled in confusion.

Peanut sent a volley of rifle fire into his raptor's centre mass. He wasn't thinking about trigger discipline, the sheer terror and absurdity of the moment causing him to hold down the trigger. His first few shots flew straight and true, but he soon lost control of the rifle.

The raptor roared in rage as the bullets tore into it. It pitched backwards, knocking a chair flying into Peanut with its thrashing tail. The soldier had the wind knocked out of him as the plush guest chair smashed him into the wall.

Ashan shifted his aim, going for the Utahraptor's legs. He sent a concentrated burst of fire into what he guessed was the knee of the creature. It had the desired effect. The thing's leg was cut out from under it in mid-charge. It landed on its belly and continued to slide forward, its jaws gnashing as it roared in pain.

"Move!" Alexa screamed.

She continued to pull the trigger as she moved, aiming for an opening between the raptor in the middle and the one on the right. Ashan pushed the two scientists along with her. The three of them started to run. Jaws filled with teeth snapped at them, barely missing Lizzie's arm.

Behind them, Ashan was helping the dazed Peanut to his feet. The man's vision was blurred at its edges, blood leaked from a wound on his head, and it felt as if bile was surging up from his guts, forcing its way through his oesophagus.

Ashan ejected his empty magazine, barely hearing it clatter to the floor as he slammed a fresh one home and picked a target. The dinosaur in the middle, which seemed to be the leader of the pack, was going after Alexa and the scientists. The one he'd shot was still writhing and thrashing about on the floor.

But Peanut's target was coming head on. Ashan tried to bring his rifle to bear, but the thing was already in the air, diving towards him. He closed his eyes to brace for impact when he was suddenly yanked backwards out of the way.

Peanut pulled Ashan back out of the monster's path, causing him to lose his footing and hit the floor. He slid along the smooth surface for a couple of feet before coming to a stop. Peanut tried to dive with him, but his injury made his movements slow, sluggish, his body refusing to respond as it should.

The raptor pounced, its jaws closing tight around his arm. A wave of intense agony flooded his senses, causing his vision to go red. He screamed, the pain unlike anything he had ever experienced before. Blood poured from the creature's jaw on the floor as it started to swing its head wildly, intent on ripping the arm from its socket.

Peanut was lifted off his feet and slammed into the wall. His vision darkened, his body unable to take the strain, his brain screaming at him to pass out to prevent his senses from overloading. Weakly, he tried to lift his rifle, only to let a few shots off into the floor.

The creature jumped in surprise as the bullets ripped its main claw off. Screeching in pain, it opened its jaws.

Peanut fell to the floor in a heap. The thing was hopping about, limping, trying to comprehend what had just happened.

The raptor Ashan had shot was still writhing on the floor, throwing chairs and breaking tables as it tried to stand on its ruined leg. Debris were being flung every which way. A chair sailed over Ashan's head into the wall, shattering into a thousand shards of plastic.

He rose to a crouch and fired at the Utahraptor that was bearing down on the wounded Peanut. The thing's eye disintegrated in a geyser of crimson as the bullets hit it. It threw its head from side to side, showering the room with its blood as it roared.

Ashan was already up and moving, running over to Peanut. He grabbed the wounded man by his vest and ran, dragging him behind. He heard gunfire ahead.

Alexa was pumping rounds in the pursuing dinosaur, but her bullets seemed to have little effect. Feathers and blood flew everywhere, yet all it seemed to do was piss the thing off. She turned to run, intending to head for the door that the scientists were already hiding behind. Lizzie was beckoning her, screaming to run faster.

A glance over Alexa's shoulder told her why. The lead raptor had gotten over its pain and was heading straight for her. The big brute was thankfully hindered by the furniture that littered the room. But then she saw Ashan and Peanut behind the thing.

Alexa spun on her heels, ejecting her spent magazine and slamming a fresh one home as she sprinted straight towards the Utahraptor. The thing's eyes gleamed, confusion and hunger colliding in its skull. This was the first time prey had ever run *towards* it.

She held her weapon out as she ran, aiming for the head but holding fire. Her eyes locked with the raptor's. Some animal instinct screamed at her to turn around, to flee, but she ignored it and kept going.

Behind the Utahraptor, Ashan watched in horrified confusion. He had no idea what she was doing, but he said a prayer under his breath for her safety as she played chicken with a fucking dinosaur.

Alexa was five feet away now. Another second before the thing had its jaws around her throat. But she swerved right, keeping her weapon aimed at the raptor's head. It couldn't change course, instead speeding past her. She opened fire just at the right moment, the muzzle of her weapon mere inches from the dinosaur's head.

Her muzzle spat fire. Rounds impacted the raptor's head in quick succession, some going straight into its eye and through its brain. It died in seconds, falling face-first onto the floor and sliding a few feet more before finally coming to a stop.

Alexa kept going all the way to the two soldiers. She bent and grabbed Peanut's vest. Together, she and Ashan sprinted towards the door, dragging the wounded man with them as they went.

Behind them, the remaining Utahraptors screamed in pain, confusion, and anger. When they were through the door, Lizzie and Waite slammed it shut. Waite hit a big red button beside the door, there was a whooshing sound, and a big metallic thunk, then silence.

"Hermetically sealed," he said, falling back against the door.

Only Lizzie heard him. Alexa and Ashan were too busy trying to save Peanut's life.

CHAPTER 20

Half the floor was just gone. And half of the next few floors. Something had torn a massive, gaping hole through several levels, leaving nothing but ruin behind. Pipes and electrical wires hung loose. Water rained down below. Sparks fizzled. Smoke drifted upwards from below.

De Vries stood on the precipice and looked down at a mass of rubble and debris that had piled up several levels below.

"What the *fok*?" he breathed.

As he stared, he found himself pitching forward. His bad leg just gave out, the pain and stress getting too much for it. And he was falling forwards, heading straight for his death, the rubble below rushing up towards him.

But that didn't happen.

Suddenly the world went the other way in a blur. Everything went backwards fast as De Vries saw the floor, the walls, then the ceiling rush past his field of vision. He hit the ground, the impact jarring the scene, his head slamming into the floor hard enough to jostle his brain. When the stars had finally cleared, he saw Monroe's face looking down at him.

"About time you told me what's wrong with your leg, old man," the lieutenant said, offering a hand.

De Vries took it. Teller was sitting in the corner, Janelle next to him. His face was contorted in pain, but he wasn't making a sound.

"Old war injury," De Vries said, "plays up now and then."

"Looks like we have something in common," Teller quipped. "Except I don't think I'll be moving very far anytime soon, Lieutenant."

"Doesn't look like there's anywhere to move to," Monroe said as he surveyed the damage. "What the fuck happened here?"

"A really big portal would be my guess," De Vries said. "Might account for all that shaking we kept feeling. *Fok* knows how we're going to get past it."

"Teller and I can stay here," Janelle said. "You two try to find a way down. It's safe enough."

De Vries stamped the ground a few times. "Seems sturdy, for now."

"I ain't going anywhere, man," Teller said. "Trust me, Lieutenant, I'm better off here. Take Janelle, though. I'll be okay on my own."

Monroe shook his head. "I won't leave you here alone. The marine stays."

"Thank you, sir," Janelle said.

"You up to the climb, old man?"

De Vries shrugged. "No choice, hey? Besides, I think I see a way to do this. We can go floor by floor, use the rubble as stepping stones. Look how everything is sort of cut out in a terrace-like pattern."

Monroe nodded. "Sounds like a plan. We've only got a few hours left before this place disintegrates, so we better hustle. Teller, Janelle, we'll be back for you."

"I know, man," Teller said. "Just look after yourself. I know how you get when I'm not there to watch your back."

"I'll do my best," Monroe said with a smirk. "Shall we?"

De Vries slung his rifle over his shoulder. He gave Teller and Janelle a thumbs up, then nodded to Monroe. It was time for a spot of mountaineering.

The first bit was easy. The wreckage of their floor had collected in a pile on the floor below, meaning that all they had to do was hop down. Monroe went first to test it, then nodded for De Vries to follow. They then clambered down the pile, kicking up concrete dust and knocking bits of masonry out of the way as they did so.

For the next two floors, it was much the same, except that once they had to use a pile of tables and chairs that made for a less sturdy platform. It wobbled and quavered under their feet, threatening to give way at any moment.

After that treacherous climb, De Vries needed a breather. He popped a pill when Monroe was busy searching for their way down. The sound of hissing pipes could be heard all around. Somewhere, a big water piper had burst, creating an indoor waterfall that sent water cascading down to the floors below.

"Climb gets harder from here," Monroe said.

"I didn't expect any less, *boet*," De Vries said. "This *bleddie* day doesn't feel like letting up, hey?"

"It never does. Although, we did come into this expecting it to be a weird one."

"True. But dinosaurs weird? Inter-dimensional portals weird? *Fok*. If I'd known I'd have packed my elephant gun."

"It's a new experience, that's for sure."

De Vries nodded. "*Ja*, and I can't help but be glad for parts of it. We just have to get out of here alive."

Monroe was about to comment when De Vries held up his hand to silence him. Some kind of screech echoed through the cavernous space. They weren't alone.

CHAPTER 21

"Hold him down!" Ashan demanded.

Lizzie and Alexa were trying their best to restrain Peanut, who was writhing on the floor in agony. His forearm was shredded, looking as if he had put it in a blender, the hand hanging limp at the end of it. There was blood everywhere.

Ashan pulled a first aid kit out of his vest and ripped it open. He grabbed a tourniquet, tying it tight just above Peanut's elbow. The man cried out in pain as it bit down hard into his skin. The effect was immediate, the flow of dark red blood slowing.

Hands slick and sticky, Ashan frantically pulled alcohol and morphine from his pack. He jammed the syringe into Peanut's upper arm, sending the opiate straight into the man's bloodstream to try and ease his pain. The alcohol he poured over the wound, doing his best to sterilise it.

Peanut screamed loud, bucking upwards and almost throwing Lizzie into the wall behind her.

"Hang in there, brother," Ashan said. "Just don't move your arm!"

The blood was making it hard to work. Things kept slipping out of his grip. He wiped his hands on his pants, trying to get enough of it off to bandage the wound effectively.

He started to wrap the white field dressing around the arm. It was soon stained crimson, the clean white a distant memory in seconds. Ashan continued to wrap the arm, heedless of Peanut's grunts of agony.

Eventually he was done. He tied off the bandage and sat back. Alexa and Lizzie let go of the wounded man. The morphine had started to take effect or shock had set in. Either way, Peanut had calmed down, no longer squirming on the floor.

"I smell smoke," Waite said.

Alexa looked up. She sniffed the air, detecting the acrid stench of burning plastic in the air.

"I smelled it earlier," she said, "before we were attacked."

They looked around at their new surroundings, which turned out to be a maze of hallways and paths leading this way and that. The smoke was coming from somewhere within, but they couldn't see it.

"What is on this floor?" Alexa asked. "Anything hazardous?"

"Nothing," Lizzie answered, "it's just offices and rec rooms. No labs here."

Alexa stood, wiping the blood off on her pants. She walked to a corner and peered around, looking for any signs of the fire. Her ears heard something else. A distinct clicking, the sound a dog made as it skittered down a passage.

Claws on tiles, she thought.

"We've got company," she said, making her way back to the others. "How do we get off this floor?"

"There should be an emergency staircase at the other end," Lizzie said. "We just head through the offices."

"Okay. Waite, Lizzie? I want you two to carry Peanut." Alexa bent and picked up the man's rifle. "Ashan, you're on point with me. Move slow, keep your eyes open, don't make a sound."

Peanut groaned as Waite and Lizzie hefted him up, supporting his weight between them. While Waite grumbled, Lizzie was careful not to touch his ruined arm. Blood was seeping through the bandage. She knew that if he didn't get help soon then he was sure to die.

Ashan stood up with difficulty, the fatigue already hitting his body. It was seeping into his bones as the stresses of the day began to take their toll. Tackling dinosaurs was hard work, even for a SEAL.

Eventually he was upright. He checked his rifle to make it sure it was cocked and locked, then nodded to Alexa.

"You're one stone-cold badass," he said to her.

She gave him a slight smile.

"I try."

As they advanced, the lights started to flicker. Ashan looked up at them, desperately hoping that they wouldn't go out. They did. The room was plunged into darkness.

Alexa and Ashan clicked the flashlights attached to their weapons on. Blinding white light filled the corridor once more. Something skittered off into the darkness, caught in the beam for less than a second.

"You see that?" Alexa asked quietly.

Ashan nodded. They continued to move. Whatever it was, it had disappeared around the corner to the left, which also happened to be the only way out. Alexa signalled for the other three to wait just as she and Ashan reached the corner.

They took each, each taking one side of the small corridor beyond. It continued for another few feet then ended in a T-junction. The floor was plush carpet and muffled their footsteps.

Ashan was sure he could see smoke at the junction. Faint wisps of it that the beam of his flashlight picked up. The smell of it was intensifying as well. A harsh chemical smell that burned the back of his throat.

In another few steps, Alexa and Ashan were at the T-junction. Ashan took left, Alexa right. They both stepped out at the same time, searching for threats. Alexa's beam fell on a room filled with dense black smoke. From somewhere within came the faint crackling of a fire.

Ashan found himself looking at another corridor with two doors leading off of it. Both were open. A rough, circular section of the carpet was missing from the floor. His thoughts turned to the clacking of claws.

Alexa motioned to the other three to advance while Ashan kept his side covered. She stopped them when they were halfway there, jogging up to talk. She pulled her hard-wearing phone and brought up the map.

"It's as I feared," she said. "Our way through is blocked by a lot of smoke. There's a fire somewhere too. Smells like plastic is burning. Any way we can get the fire system going? Maybe vent the room?"

Lizzie and Waite gently lowered Peanut to the floor. They sat him against the wall so that his back was supported. He groaned, but he looked like his head was clearing.

"There should be a system on each floor that can vent smoke and put out fires," Waite said. "I don't know why it hasn't triggered. Give me the phone."

Alexa handed it to him. He looked at the screen for a moment, then started to manipulate the map with his fingers before stopping, pinching to zoom in, and handing it back.

"That room there," he said. "It will have the controls in it. Should be a big box on the way. Open it up and push a button. Easy as that. Since scientists don't work on this floor, we wanted to make it so that even a luddite could operate the thing. Even your soldiers shouldn't have any trouble."

"Fuck," Alexa swore. "We still have to go through the smoke. Wait here and look after him."

She jogged back up to Ashan to explain the situation. He considered their options.

"We may have hostiles up this way," he said. "And I don't want to risk too many people in that smoke. You stay with Peanut and the scientists. I'll activate the anti-fire system. No arguments. I can handle myself and the civvies need protection."

"Okay," Alexa said, "but you be careful."

"Always."

Ashan took the phone and they checked their comms. Still no joy. Only static, even between them. Alexa pulled out her regular phone. There was no signal, but it looked like she had a text from her boy. She shoved the phone back in her pocket, unwilling to think about her son at the moment.

"Watch that damn corridor," Ashan said. "I got a bad feeling about it."

He walked back to the junction. He studied the map for a moment, memorising the route. Then, he pulled a handkerchief out of his pocket, soaked it through with water from his canteen, and tied it around his nose and mouth. That done, he got down on his hands and knees so that he was below the smoke before beginning to crawl.

Even though he was below the smoke, his eyes still burned. It was thick, black, and smelled of chemicals. Briefly, he wondered how carcinogenic it was, but pushed the thoughts away, instead focusing on going the right way.

The floor was a mess. The office had been abandoned in a hurry, leaving debris everywhere. Broken cups, stationery, computers, all kinds of stuff littered the carpet. He noticed that a few patches of it had worryingly dark stains.

A crash from up ahead stopped him in his tracks. He blinked, trying to see through the tears in his eyes. He could feel the smoke getting into his lungs. There was something in front of him. More than one, he realised in horror.

They were little, numerous, and they were running straight towards him.

CHAPTER 22

"Is that what I think it is?" Monroe asked, staring upwards.

"Pterodactyl," De Vries said.

Several massive winged reptiles, their skin various shades of green, were appearing from an alcove above them. They screeched as they took flight and were circling as best they could in the confined space, their beaks snapping open and shut as they flew.

De Vries had a sinking feeling in the pit of his stomach. Their flight pattern resembled that of carnivorous birds circling their prey.

"We have to hurry."

"Follow me then, old man."

The next part of the climb down required a drop of a few feet onto a pile of tables below. Monroe went first, landing well, his training taking over. He bent his knees slightly, worried that the structure of debris wouldn't hold. It did. He nodded up to De Vries.

De Vries didn't give himself time to think – he just jumped, preparing himself as much as he could for the shock of the landing. He hit the platform, a jolt of pain running up his leg. He almost lost his balance, recovering at the last moment.

Then the structure gave way beneath his feet.

It started when a small piece of wood cracked in two, shifting the balance of everything above it. The world tilted sideways at a Dutch angle for De Vries. Briefly, he was weightless, then he was tumbling with all the rubble around him.

Concrete dust forced its way up his nostrils, his hands scrabbled for purchase, and bits and pieces of masonry rained down around him. He couldn't see anything through his dust-filled eyes except a blur of movement.

Someone grabbed his hand, the grip firm. He was yanked to a sudden stop, still coughing and spluttering. The rubble continued to tumble and fall, some of it careening off the edge and down to the lower floors, where it landed with a massive splash. The burst pipes had flooded the floors below, forming a lake of dirty water.

"I got you," Monroe said as he hauled De Vries away from the edge that he had been perilously close to.

De Vries coughed some more before hacking up a ball of phlegm. He spat it over the edge, taking some small satisfaction in hearing it splash into the waters below.

"I am so *fokken* tired of falling," he said.

Monroe laughed. A shriek from above cut it off. Both men looked up to see one of the pterodactyls break formation and dive towards them.

The lieutenant leaped out the way in time, but De Vries was too slow and in too much pain to move fast enough. He felt the thing's claws bite into his shoulder as it lifted him off his feet, his rifle still slung over his back.

He didn't waste any time, making a quick grab for his knife as the thing started pulling him towards its nest.

Monroe picked himself up off the floor to see De Vries being carried off. He raised his weapon, only to notice another pterodactyl make a dive for him. He moved targets and opened fire in one smooth movement.

There was a puff of red mist, a screech, and the animal veered off to the side to crash into a floor above in a shower of dust. Monroe shifted his aim once more, setting his sights on the reptile that had De Vries in its grip.

The older man was still struggling to grab a hold of his knife. The thing was jerking him around as it flew and its claws dug painfully into his shoulder. He could feel the wound from earlier opening up, blood soaking into his clothes once more.

Finally, his fingers gripped the knife. De Vries wrenched it out of its sheath and used it to slash furiously at the pterodactyl's claws. The dinosaur gave an almighty yell as the knife pierced its flesh, its claws releasing their grasp in the same moment.

And for what seemed like the hundredth time that day, De Vries was falling. That now familiar weightless sensation, the feeling of his stomach being left behind as his body went downwards, the terror of realising what he had done. All of this rushed through his body and mind until, seconds later, he hit the water.

The shock of the impact knocked the wind out of him. He opened his mouth involuntarily, gulping for air but getting water instead. He choked, desperately trying to orient himself in the murky liquid that surrounded him.

De Vries' lungs were now screaming at him to get air into him, to spit out the water that had forced its way down his throat. He kicked his feet, attempting to propel himself towards the surface and the sweet oxygen above.

Monroe watched De Vries fall, thinking for one terrifying moment that the man was dead. Then he hit the water. The lieutenant was about to dive in after the old man when more hungry calls from above him drew his attention upwards.

Three of the creatures were heading straight for him, sharp, vicious-looking beaks glinting evilly in the artificial light. Monroe didn't think, instead acting on instinct and muscle memory that had been ingrained in him from years of being an operator.

The rifle raised, the stick finding that sweet spot in his shoulder where he could support the recoil. He took aim, his finger tightening on the trigger. The rifle kicked, spat fire, sending hot lead death towards its target.

Monroe didn't wait to see the hit. He adjusted his aim, squeezed, and fired again. Then he moved, diving backwards to ensure that the things didn't tear into him as they landed.

De Vries' head broke the surface with a splash. He hacked and coughed and spluttered, his body trying to expel the putrid water from his lungs. His face whipped to the side, trying to find a way out. All the time, the rifle on his back threatened to drag him downwards once more.

Finding a bank, he swam towards it. He could feel the fatigue setting in as his body threatened to give out. His muscles wanted to relax, to give up and let him sink slowly to the bottom. Drawing on energy reserves he hadn't needed for years, he continued to paddle.

One of the pterodactyls was dead in the air, the bullets having caught it in its lizard brain. The thing just stopped flapping and drifted downwards, smashing into a pile of rubble below.

The second reptile angled itself slightly, instead taking the bullets in the shoulder. It roared in rage and tried to fly faster, heading directly for its prey.

The third one just peeled off, scared off by the gunshots. It flew higher and higher. Monroe watched it just long enough to confirm that it was no longer a threat, then turned his attention back to the injured animal that was heading right for him.

Once again, his muscles took over. Rifle, shoulder, squeeze. The dry click of an empty chamber.

Monroe cursed his rookie mistake as he dove to the left. The reptile crashed into the ground where his body had been mere seconds before. Its wing caught the lieutenant, shoving him sideways with one powerful flap. The momentum from his dive and the added force of the blow pushed him further than he intended to go.

He slid along the floor towards the edge, his hands scrabbling for purchase. The dust and debris on the floor did nothing to hinder his slide as he careened towards almost certain death. His feet went over the edge, then his pelvis, his stomach, his chest, and finally – his hand clasped around a protruding piece of rebar.

Monroe was jerked to a stop, his shoulder almost popping out of its socket as he came to a sudden halt. He didn't hesitate to thank any Gods, he just raised his other hand to grab onto the ledge as quickly as he could. The lieutenant was painfully aware of the lack of solid ground under his legs as he attempted to heave himself upwards.

De Vries hauled himself out of the water onto the floor. His eyes stung, his muscles were aching more than they ever had, his lungs burned, and he was coughing and puking water. But he was alive. In the back of his mind, he wondered how an entire floor had been flooded.

Perhaps the portal brought the water with it?

The thought brought a fresh wave of coughs. He didn't want to get some prehistoric disease from dirty water. To survive all this and die of Jurassic dysentery would be the cruellest of fates.

De Vries got up on his knees, forcing himself to puke up whatever water he had swallowed. His throat stung from the bile, but he felt it was better out than in.

"You okay down there, old man?" Monroe called from above.

De Vries looked up. The man was dusty and bloody, but alive. De Vries figured that he looked like a drowned rat. He gave the lieutenant a thumbs up.

"Roger that. I'll be right down. Try not to fall off that ledge too, okay?"

De Vries flipped him off, but nodded weakly.

CHAPTER 23

Instinct took over as Ashan pulled his pistol from its holster. He aimed above the creatures, not wanting to hurt something so small, and fired. The little dinosaurs, which looked like they had stepped right out of a movie from the 90s, scattered at the shots.

Ashan realised his mistake almost immediately. He looked left and right, knowing they were now coming from all directions. He started to crawl faster, focusing on getting to the panel that would vent the smoke.

His eyes were stinging. The acrid taste was now working its way down his throat towards his lungs. It wouldn't be long before he started to succumb to smoke inhalation.

A Compsognathus came from his left, leaping onto his back. Tiny jaws bit down on the exposed flesh of his neck. Ashan swiped at it, knocking the Compy off, but not before it took a chunk with it.

More of the creatures rushed past, letting out tiny shrieks as they did. Some attacked him, but most just ran, seemingly in blind terror.

Ashan kept moving, ignoring the pain in the back of his neck. Ignoring the hot, sticky blood that flowed down onto the floor.

What scared them so much? he wondered as he moved.

The handkerchief across his face was starting to dry out. He coughed once, twice, the smoke forcing its way down his throat and into his lungs. His eyes were red, bloodshot, and watering, his vision almost a blur.

But Ashan kept moving as fast as he could. He knew that if he didn't get to the panel, he was dead. There was no going back.

Two more Compys appeared out of nowhere, leaping onto his back and attacking him in a blind panic. They snatched and nibbled and swiped at his back. He heard cloth tear, felt a sharp stinging pain on his arm.

Ashan fired his pistol again, sending a round towards the ceiling. One of the Compys screeched before fleeing into the smoke. The other stayed, latching onto him with its vicious little jaws.

The SEAL ignored it, instead pushing forwards towards the panel. It was close now. He could feel it. Then he saw it – a bright red light in the smoke, drawing him towards it.

The Compy on his back gave up, leaping towards the floor and skittering off. Ashan started coughing and hacking, his lungs burning from the smoke. Tears flowed down his cheeks like a river, smearing clear lines down the soot on his face.

He stood, feeling along the wall for the junction box. His hands touched it and he wrenched it open. Through his blurred vision, he could only barely see the buttons in front of him. Ashan took a chance, slamming his hand onto one of them.

A tense second of silence passed before he heard fans start up somewhere above him. Slowly, the smoke started to clear. The sprinklers came on suddenly, soaking him through.

Ashan collapsed to the floor. He ripped off the handkerchief and turned his face upwards, letting the water wash out his eyes and run down his face. It felt clean, fresh, amazing, especially after the smoke.

He coughed and spat, trying to clear his throat. It had been rubbed raw by the smoke. His lungs still felt like they were on fire.

Over the sound of the sprinklers and the whirring fans, he heard something. It sounded familiar, but it took him a while to place it. When he did, he grabbed at his rifle.

It was the sound of claws on a tiled floor.

**

"That your son?" Lizzie asked.

Alexa looked up from the picture on her phone and nodded.

"Javier," she said. "He's twelve."

"Aw," Lizzie said awkwardly, "he looks… cute."

Alexa laughed. "Not a fan of kids?"

"Who is?" Peanut asked, his voice faint.

"Parents, mostly," Lizzie replied. "But no. Not that I expect Javier to be bad or anything, I just…"

"It's okay," Alexa said. "I never thought I'd have one. Javier was a surprise."

Waite snorted. "Can't have been that unexpected, considering what you had to do to get him."

Lizzie gave him a look, then continued. "You and your partner weren't trying?"

Alexa laughed. "In my job, partners are who you work with, not who you spend your free time with. No. He was a guy I spent a month or two with. He pays child support but is happy letting me do all the heavy lifting."

"Real stand-up guy," Peanut said.

"Not as bad as some," Alexa said pointedly.

"How do you do it? The whole single mother thing?" Lizzie asked, hugging herself against the chill of the air conditioner.

"You just do. As with anything else in life, you do what you need to do."

Gunshots echoed down the corridor suddenly. Alexa leapt to her feet and ran down to the junction. A group of small Compys ran past her, snapping at her ankles as they went.

"You think he's okay?" Lizzie asked.

Alexa didn't answer. She wanted to run to help Ashan, but it was pointless. The smoke was too thick. She'd be a casualty in no time, and she couldn't leave the civilians without protection.

"He'll be fine," Peanut said, hauling himself up. "He's a SEAL."

"What are you doing?" Lizzie asked. "Sit down! You need to rest."

Peanut pulled out his handgun. "Fuck that. I heard something. Listen."

They all kept quiet. More gunshots came from Ashan's position. Then silence. Alexa listened hard, hearing it thirty seconds later. As if on cue, the dinosaurs that had run past her earlier skittered back down the corridor.

"What the–" Lizzie exclaimed, jumping back to avoid the creatures.

Alexa looked down the opposite corridor, watching for movement. Behind her came a mechanical roar as Ashan turned on the fans. She resisted the urge to look back, instead focusing on the darkness at the end of the hall.

She could hear movement ahead but she couldn't see anything. Silently, she prayed that Ashan would hurry up so that they could get out of there. She was certain that something big and dangerous was hiding in the dark.

CHAPTER 24

"They okay down there?" Teller asked anxiously.

Janelle looked over the edge, one hand braced on the wall beside her. They'd heard the fight between De Vries, Monroe, and the flying beasts. She saw De Vries flip the lieutenant off.

"They're fine," she said, returning to Teller's side.

"Thank fuck. I ain't feeling very useful right now."

"Not like you have a choice, man."

Teller sighed. He adjusted his leg and grimaced. It was a bad break, he knew it. He'd had his fair share of broken bones, from stress fractures to clean snaps. This one felt like the latter.

"I hate not being useful," he said at last.

"Happens to all of us. Check this out."

Janelle lifted her shirt to reveal a criss-crossing mess of scar tissue on her abdomen. It was puckered and nasty, running along her otherwise smooth flesh like some kind of weird map of a foreign country.

"This shit put me out of action," she said. "IED went off and my vehicle got hit. Surgeons did what they could, but you know. Reason I ain't a Marine no more."

"Once a Marine, always a Marine, Marine," Teller said. "That's a gnarly scar though."

"Yeah. The girls love it."

Teller laughed. "I'll bet. My wife hates them. Says they reminds her of all the shit I go through. When we get out of this one, I'll have a hell of a story for her."

"We both will, man. Ain't like this shit happens every day."

"Did you know what was going on in these labs?"

Janelle shook her head. "Nah, man. We were paid well and told nothing. Same as the Marines."

"How the hell have they hidden all of this in the middle of New York?"

"Easy. No one looks at the obvious stuff. Just another building in a city."

"With way more weird shit going on inside. Fucking dinosaurs, man."

"Not what I expected when I came to work this morning," Janelle said with a laugh.

"If this doesn't get classified up the ass, my kids will love this story."

"Who else will believe it? We come out of this talking about dinos and they'll stick all our asses in the loony bin."

"I dunno, man," Teller mused. "Padded cell looks pretty good right about now. Better than this damn corridor at any rate."

"Amen, brother."

Teller looked at the stairwell door. "We need a way to clear the stairwell. I can't let the others suffer through this without me. Besides, we're gonna need a way to get downstairs."

Janelle thought for a moment. "I think I have an idea."

***

"At least the ladder is still attached, hey?" De Vries said.

Monroe grunted. He and the older man were standing at the edge of the elevator, which may as well have been the precipice of a mountain. Darkness, thick and soupy, stretched away below.

The ladder De Vries had noted was indeed still bolted to the wall. The only issue was that it was on the other side of the elevator shaft, with a good few feet of inky blackness between them and it.

"This day isn't going to get any easier, is it?" Monroe said.

De Vries sighed heavily. "Guess not. That's our only way down. Unless we want to go for a swim to try and find another way."

Monroe looked over his shoulder at the indoor swimming pool that De Vries had been thrown into. There was a chance that they could dive underwater to discover a door to the lower levels. But it was a slim chance. Even if they did find one, they had no way to get it open.

"Can you make the jump, old man?" Monroe asked.

De Vries massaged his leg, feeling the damaged muscle underneath the skin as he did so. "No choice, my friend."

"Okay." Monroe handed his rifle to De Vries. "I'll go first, you hand over the rifles once I'm across. If you have any trouble on the jump, I'll grab you."

"Roger that, Lieutenant."

Monroe walked back from the edge, turned, took a breath, and then sprinted forward. He reached the edge of the shaft and leapt, his hands outstretched in front of him. He grabbed at the ladder, closing around the rungs in a death-grip as the momentum carried him into the wall.

The impact almost winded him, but Monroe managed to keep his grip. He got his boots on the rungs below, finally stabilising himself and taking a deep breath.

"Easy," he breathed.

De Vries looked at him incredulously. Monroe smiled, then motioned for the rifles. The old hunter passed them over and the lieutenant slung both over his back.

"Your turn, old man."

De Vries massaged his leg a bit, then stretched it out. The pain was there, gently nagging at him, telling him that something was wrong. He knew it was going to get worse. But for now, it was just bearable.

He judged the distance, backed up a few feet, then started his run up. As he went, he felt the building start to shake under his feet. That familiar feeling of electricity in the air. The hairs on his arms stood on end.

De Vries kept going. Kept running. Keeping his focus on the jump, he hoped that the portal wouldn't open anywhere close.

He reached the precipice and jumped, pushing off with his feet. His leg protested, almost giving out underneath him. But he made the leap and was sailing through the air towards the ladder.

De Vries had a moment of sheer terror when he thought he wasn't going to make it. The air around him was crackling with energy, a pale blue light had illuminated the elevator shaft. His hands were an inch away from the ladder. He was going to make it.

And he would have. If the portal hadn't opened right in front of him at the last second.

CHAPTER 25

"Get him up," Alexa hissed.

Lizzie started to haul Peanut to his feet. Waite just stood there, seemingly frozen with fear. Lizzie slapped his arm to get his attention.

Alexa kept her eyes on the T-junction. The clicking of claws against the floor was getting closer. She leaned in close to Peanut.

"Got any flashbangs?" she asked.

He nodded. He was looking pale and worn-out, but he used his uninjured hand to point. Alexa pulled one of the cylinders loose and shoved it in her pocket.

"We move towards Ashan's position," she whispered.

Everyone nodded. Behind them they heard the squeaks and shrieks of the Compys as they ran about.

Alexa took point, going forward weapon first. She moved as quickly as she could, careful not to trip or kick any of the rubble on the floor. Peanut let out a groan as the two scientists started to carry him forward.

The clicking stopped. Whatever was in the corridor ahead growled, low and menacing. It sounded big, probably another Utahraptor, separated from the others. Or something worse.

It was only a few feet to the junction now. Alexa glanced right, making sure it was clear. She heard what sounded like rain. The sprinklers, she realised. Water was trickling down around the corner.

Five feet...

Three...

Alexa rounded the corner with her weapon up and ready to fire. All she could see was darkness down the left side. Pitch black. She motioned the others to keep moving.

Goosebumps started to break out across her flesh. Her arm hairs stood on end. The now familiar crackle of energy in the air signalled another portal.

At the same time, the huge jaws of a Utahraptor appeared out of the darkness. Its intelligent, hungry eyes caught sight of Alexa. The jaws opened, emitting a roar of hunger, anger, and confusion.

Alexa's finger tightened on the trigger a second too late. The thing was already in the air, pushing off the ground with its powerful hind legs. It was flying towards her, seemingly in defiance of physics. Moving forward too fast and too high for something so big.

Her volley of shots went underneath the creature, pinging off something in the darkness beyond. She willed her legs to move, to power her out the way of the thing's reach, but the spectacle was too incredible. Her brain shut down, leaving her rooted to the spot.

Behind her, Lizzie screamed, loud and harsh and commanding. Yelling at her to move.

It was a foot away now, the whole scene moving in intense slow motion in Alexa's mind. She could see every tooth in the creature's mouth. A chunk of torn human flesh dangled out the left side.

There was a sudden explosion of harsh blue light, a portal opening right in front of Alexa. The creature roared in surprise, but it was too late. It hurtled through the portal into whatever lay beyond.

Alexa realised she had been holding her breath. She let it out in one big gasp. She sucked in air like her life depended on it. A wave of unbelievable relief flowed through her. The emotion was so strong that she teared up.

Lizzie laughed. A nervous bark of laughter that echoed down the now empty corridors. Peanut smiled. Waite looked curious.

"That was close," Peanut whispered, but Alexa heard him.

She turned to smile at the group. To crack a joke to break the tension. Something that would relieve the intense knot in her stomach.

Her face fell when she saw what was behind them. Ashan was backing up towards them, soaking wet and firing his rifle.

"Contact!" he shouted above the gunfire.

"Fuck," Alexa swore, raising her weapon.

CHAPTER 26

De Vries landed hard. He tried to roll with it, tucking his shoulder as he hit the ground, but it was almost impossible. He ended up flat on his back, winded, staring at a clear blue sky through a canopy far above his head.

Something heavy landed on the ground beside him. He rolled sideways in a panic, not sure what it was. He searched desperately for threats, wondering whether to start running. There was no need. It was his weapon, chucked into the portal by Monroe before it closed.

De Vries took a breath, a slight smile on his face. It was a *kak* day alright, but at least he had a gun. He picked it up, then stood to take in his surroundings.

He was in the middle of a forest. Huge trees towered above him, their trunks as thick as the baobab trees back at home. He could hear sounds of life everywhere, from the rustling of tiny creatures in the undergrowth to the squawk of creatures overhead.

"What the hell do I do now?" he wondered aloud.

They had been getting lucky with the portals so far, getting zapped out of the past almost as soon as they were zapped into it. But De Vries had no idea how long that luck would last. For all he knew, it could have already run out.

The forest he now stood in could be his home for a while. Or it could be a pit stop. And then there was the question of how his presence would affect the future, if at all.

He remembered that his granddaughter liked science fiction movies. He'd watched a few with her. And the only constant with the time travel ones was that they could never bloody decide what the rules were.

De Vries turned in a slow circle, trying to get his bearings. The sheer density of the trees and ferns on the forest floor made it hard to see more than a few meters ahead. But he did see that the terrain rose slightly to the south.

The first rule of survival situations was always to get to high ground. Find out where you were, then focus on getting out.

The old hunter sighed. His leg was really sore now, the fall through the portal having done it no favours. He felt his pockets for the pain meds that he carried and held the bottle up to his eyes.

Three pills rattled around in the clear plastic tube. He shook one out, swallowed, and cursed his leg. It seemed to be playing up more and more these days. Aging was doing its work on his body, De Vries reckoned.

He started south, moving as quickly as he could while still keeping his eyes and ears open. The forest life seemed to want to steer clear of him for now, but there was no telling when that would change.

Somewhere in the distance, something roared. It sounded big and powerful. De Vries quickened his pace, hoping that he was getting away from whatever it was. He was pleased to find himself heading up some sort of hill, the trees thinning as he climbed

Ten minutes later, panting, sweating and in pain, De Vries found himself on top of a large hill that seemed to be in the centre of the forest. Trees stretched out for miles in all directions, some so tall that he could barely see over them. The air was cleaner and fresher than he had ever experienced before.

De Vries sat down, balancing his rifle in his lap. Another roar echoed through the forest. He didn't have many options, he realised.

If he headed east, he knew that he could at least get out of the forest, because he could just see flat terrain in that direction. But that was going to take a lot of walking. And he had a feeling that that's where the big roaring creature was.

He sighed heavily, the pain, fatigue and frustration weighing down on him like a drugged elephant. As amazing as all the things he'd seen that day were, he'd have preferred to be back in Africa, in the middle of the bush.

De Vries had always thought that he'd die on African soil. It was home. Where he was born and where he belonged. Yet here he was, probably millions of years in the past and surrounded by hostile dinosaurs.

He laughed, a genuine, from the belly guffaw that echoed down the hill into the trees below. What else could he do? Either he laughed or he gave up. So he laughed, long and loud.

When he was done, he stood, pointed himself eastwards, and started walking.

Let's hope my luck holds out, hey?

CHAPTER 27

"You watched a lot of *MacGyver* as a kid, didn't you?" Teller asked.

Janelle smiled, taking a step back to admire her hastily assembled contraption. It was comprised of a bucket, several different cleaning chemicals in very specific portions, and a makeshift lid duct taped to the top.

"What's the matter? Never seen anyone make a firebomb from scratch before?"

"Outside of the movies?" Teller asked. "No. I haven't."

"Just me then," she said. "Then again, I was a weird kid. Always trying to recreate what I saw in *MacGyver* reruns. Drove my parents nuts."

She hefted the makeshift bomb and carried it to the door, before setting it down carefully.

"You got a lighter?"

Teller fished his lighter out of his pocket and tossed it to Janelle. She pulled a strip of cloth out of her pocket, soaked it, then shoved it into the bucket through a hole she'd made in the lid. She pressed her ear against the stairwell door.

After listening for a moment, she took hold of the handle. After using the lighter to light the makeshift fuse, she pushed the door open just far enough for her to shove the bomb through. As she slammed the door shut once more, she heard the startled cries of the creatures.

Janelle ran back to Teller and they both hunkered down in the storage room, waiting for the explosion. A minute of tense silence was followed by a *whump* as the bomb detonated. Flames spat under the door. Fierce screeches of pain and surprise penetrated their ears.

It was all over in a matter of seconds. Silence fell, so complete that it made their ears ring.

"Let's see if that worked," Janelle said.

She took the rifle with her and pressed herself against the door. It was warm to the touch. The knob itself was red hot. But she didn't have to turn it. The force of the blast had rattled the door loose.

Using the barrel of the rifle, Janelle slowly pushed the door open. A wave of intense heat washed over her, followed by the acrid, nauseating stench of burning chemicals. Smoke curled around in the stairwell beyond, making bizarre patterns in the air.

Janelle swept the stairwell, trying her best not to breathe too deeply. She didn't see any sign of the black mass of creatures. They'd been scared into retreating upwards by the firebomb. She smiled.

"Looks like we're good to go," she said, just as the overhead sprinklers came on and drenched her.

* * *

Alexa's brain went into overdrive. Ashan was backing up towards her, the staccato rhythm of his rifle hammering her ear drums. Shell casings were landing on the floor, giving the whole scene a bizarrely jaunty jingle.

But whatever was coming wasn't stopping, despite the amount of lead being poured into it.

One chance.

"Flash out!" Alexa roared.

She yanked the flashbang from her pocket and tossed it over Ashan's head. The two of them turned, put their hands over their ears, and opened their mouths in preparation for the blast.

The grenade went off with an obscenely loud bang. The hallway was bathed in blinding light. Something roared in surprise, which was quickly followed by a snarl.

Alexa was already moving, grabbing the scientists, whose ears were ringing, and pushing them. Peanut got the message, and groggy though he was, did his best to urge them on.

Ashan ran back and shouted at Lizzie and Waite to run. He hefted Peanut in a fireman's carry before following, the young SEAL groaning as his arm was jostled. Alexa brought up the rear.

All of them ran their hardest, feet pounding the wet floor. The carpet squelched underneath their feet. Alexa saw a hint of something big in the corner as it thrashed around in a blind panic. She ignored it, focusing on not tripping on the sodden carpeting.

Waite was the first to reach the stairwell, his long lanky legs carrying him forward at a hell of a pace. He hit it with his shoulder and it flew open, slamming into the wall with a crash. Lizzie followed, then Ashan, and finally, Alexa, who slammed it shut behind her.

"Keep going!" she screamed.

No one needed to be told twice. They bounded down the stairs, Alexa marvelling at Ashan's strength and ability as he carried Peanut downwards.

An almighty crash echoed down the stairwell as the big dinosaur upstairs charged its way through the door. It roared, long and loud and terrifying. A sound that bounced off the walls to chill the blood.

Alexa could almost sense the frustration of the creature, because she knew it was too big to get down the stairs.

The group made it down five stories before Ashan called for a break. He put Peanut down carefully before collapsing into a sweating heap. Water still clung to his clothes, forming a little puddle under his ass.

Lizzie sucked in air hard, her hands on her knees. Waite breathed like a long-distance runner, slow and methodical. Alexa kept her rifle pointed upwards as the dinosaur continued to rage at losing its prey.

"As an *Uber* driver," Peanut said, "I'd rate you as two stars, man. Fucking terrible driving."

Ashan chuckled. "Next time you do the carrying then, asshole."

CHAPTER 28

Desert scrub stretched out before him as far as his eyes could see. In the distance, he could see massive shapes lumbering through the heat. The haze made them shimmer and dance about.

De Vries stood on the edge of the forest, gazing out at the open plain ahead. It didn't seem right that there should be a desert next to a forest. But what did he know about flora and fauna from millions of years ago?

Tracks, huge and alien to him, crisscrossed the sands. It looked like a huge variety of creatures had been through. Idly, he wondered how many of them would fancy him for a spot of lunch.

His thoughts drifted to his grandkids for a moment. If he survived this, he'd have a hell of a story for them. He could imagine their eyes lighting up in child-like amazement at his tale of time travel and dinosaurs. The thought brought a smile to his face.

"Good a reason to keep going as any," he said aloud.

The wind whistled across the plain in answer. His leg sent a shooting pain through his body. He flinched and dug another pain pill out of his pocket.

As he dry swallowed it, he considered his options. He didn't have many. Either he went out on a trek across the desert or he stayed where he was and prayed for another portal to open. Neither option was particularly appealing – not least because he had heard several critters rustling about in the forest behind him.

Unable to come to a decision, De Vries did the only thing he could do. He sat down and thought about it.

***

Monroe gripped the ladder tight and breathed in deep. After De Vries had disappeared through the portal, he'd continued down. His climb had lasted longer than he'd expected, taxing even his trained, athletic build. It had been a long fucking day.

Darkness stretched out above and below him. It was seemingly infinite, giving him no sense of how much further he had to go until he reached the basement.

The muscles in his arms and legs ached something terrible. His sweat had soaked into his already sodden clothes, refusing to let them dry. He shivered as yet another draft wafted through the elevator shaft.

Monroe checked his watch. The screen was smashed beyond repair. He had no idea how long until the building exploded. Not long, he guessed, judging by the increasing frequency of the tremors that were rocking the building.

With a sigh, he continued his arduous climb. The downtime had let the various trials of the day catch up with him. Even SEALs got tired after being chased around a building by dinosaurs.

"Forty percent," he muttered to himself.

He kept his reasons for climbing at the forefront of his mind. His duty as a soldier. His empathy towards the people of the city. It all helped him keep climbing, ignoring the pain in his limbs and the burning of his lungs.

Monroe didn't have a choice. For all he knew, he was the last one of his team alive. He needed to keep going and shut off the power before the building exploded and took most of Manhattan with it.

***

"You know, I was just thinking how this day could get worse," Teller said.

The overhead sprinklers were still going. Janelle and himself were drenched to the bone. Worse still, the water that sloshed down the stairs made the journey down even more difficult.

"At least you don't have to lug your fat ass down a million fucking stairs," Janelle said. "I mean for fuck's sake, I thought SEALs were supposed to be fit."

"All muscle, Marine," Teller joked.

Janelle snorted. "If that ass of yours is all muscle, then I'm a fucking hairdresser."

They laughed. Janelle felt some of the tension leave her shoulders as the good-natured ribbing between the two of them worked its magic.

"You should just leave my ass here, Marine."

"Fuck off. Your LT wouldn't let me hear the end of it."

"That's true," Teller chuckled. "But we are on a time limit here."

"A vague one at best."

"All the more reason for you to move faster."

Janelle looked at him. Water was running down her face like a river. She could feel him wince at each step they took. His leg must have felt like it was on fire.

"I ain't gonna leave you behind," she said. "I don't wanna die alone."

It was obviously a joke. But there was a truth behind the statement that gave it weight.

"Okay then!" Teller said with a mock sigh of exasperation. "I'll babysit your ass then. Don't have to get all emotional on me. Jeez."

"Tell me about your kids. I need some cheering up."

"Ha! You think my kids will cheer you up? I bet you don't even like kids."

"Don't have to like them to find cute stories entertaining."

"Hold up, Marine," Teller said suddenly.

Janelle set him down gently. He let out a long sigh as he straightened his busted leg. The sprinklers had finally turned off, but water still ran down the stairs. The sound of it rushing past was oddly soothing.

"You good?" she asked.

Teller nodded. She could see from the way his jaw was set that the pain was getting worse. They were still in the double digits when it came to floors.

"You think the others are making progress?" Janelle asked.

Teller nodded. "I'm guessing they are. If not, it's not like we'll know much about it when the place goes boom. Can't worry about what's not in our control. You know what I'm wondering? Why haven't we found any other survivors?"

"Any survivors would be downstairs, most likely."

"But surely there'd be some security teams? As far as I know, no one made it out before the building locked down. We found a lotta bodies upstairs though. Or parts of what used to be bodies."

Janelle shrugged. "Comms went down shortly after everything went to shit. Same way yours shorted. Probably to do with all the portals."

As if on cue, the building rumbled and shook again. The sign that had the floor number on it fell from the wall and clattered to the ground.

"What's SOP for emergencies here?" Teller asked.

"Head downstairs, like I said."

"And surely they'd know about the overloading power thing in the basement?"

"One of the scientists or engineers, maybe, yeah."

"Then either they're trapped somewhere…"

"Or we're going to stumble across a lot more dead bodies before we reach the basement."

***

"How's he doing?" Alexa asked, making sure to keep her voice low.

They had made good progress downstairs, encountering no more dinosaurs. Although they'd heard strange noises from behind a few doors. They were all bone tired, so much so that even Waite had stopped complaining. Although he hadn't failed to mention that they only had about an hour before the building exploded.

"If we don't get him to a hospital soon…" Ashan replied.

Alexa looked at the ashen-faced Peanut. He was barely conscious. Lizzie was doing her best to comfort him.

"I'm thinking of splitting up," Alexa said. "You take Peanut and Lizzie to the lobby so that when the doors open, you can get them out ASAP."

"I'd rather you did that, ma'am."

She gave him a look. "You're more capable of carrying him than I am. Waite and I can move faster alone. Get to the basement, shut off the power, and get out."

"What about the dinosaurs? We're risking letting quite a few of them out once the lockdown ends, aren't we?"

"Fuck. I didn't think of that. But it's a risk we have to take. Can't let this place go super nova and wipe out the city."

"Guess we just hope for the best and plan for the worst. I tell you what. If I can find a good place for Peanut and the doc to hole up, I'll join you after getting them settled."

"Only if you can guarantee their safety."

"Agreed."

"Come on. We've got to keep moving."

Ashan nodded. He bent and hefted Peanut up once more. Lizzie stood, her eyes betraying how on edge she was. Waite looked up at Alexa.

"Good to see you're finally ready to keep moving and stop my life's work going up in smoke," he said.

"Just get up and get moving, Doctor. We're going to go on ahead. We don't have much time."

"Just the two of us?"

"Yes."

Alexa started down the stairs. Waite watched her go, not sure what to do. He looked at the SEALs.

"Better follow her, Doc. Otherwise she'll leave you behind."

He leapt to his feet and jogged down after her. Alexa didn't even look round when he came up behind her. She just hoped that he knew what to do to diffuse the massive bomb they were all sitting on.

CHAPTER 29

It felt as if he was being baked alive. The sun was beating down relentlessly, making De Vries marvel at how creatures could survive in the dessert beyond. He wouldn't have lasted more than a day, if his short scouting mission was anything to go by.

He'd only walked a hundred or so meters into the sands, hoping to see some sign that would help him get home. All he'd come across were more massive tracks. What's worse, the heat haze made it impossible to see if there was any end to the sandblasted hellscape he'd found himself in.

So he turned and headed back to the forest. His choice had been made for him. Stay put and hope that another portal opened nearby. But until then he had his basic survival needs to think about. Step one was to find water.

The smell hit his nostrils after he had taken five steps into the forest. The same scent of burning ozone that had accompanied every portal so far.

De Vries took off running. His leg protested, forcing him to limp and slowing him down. But he pushed through the agony, his teeth gritted. It wasn't long before he reached the source of the smell. And it wasn't what he'd thought it was.

Before him was a jumble of random debris, from concrete slabs to office chairs and computers. It was all piled up in a big, unnatural clearing. It seemed like the portals had made it, if the scorched trees were any indication.

De Vries noticed several bodies amongst the detritus, some human, some dinosaur, and other mutilated beyond recognition. The smell that accompanied the portals was almost overpowering. Bits of rubble still smoked.

As he took in the scene, he noticed something odd. Skirting the edge of the pile of wreckage, he came to what looked like a path leading deeper into the woods. Metal poles had been set into the ground on either side and rope strung between them.

De Vries followed the path through the trees. After five minutes of walking, he found himself in a camp of some sort.

Several white canvas tents were strung up wherever there was space. They were arranged in a loose semi-circle around a fire pit. Three logs surrounded the pit, presumably to be used as benches.

As he tried to figure out how the camp had come to be, one of the tents opened to reveal a man in jungle fatigues with a white lab coat pulled over them. His eyes widened when he noticed the old hunter.

"Thank god!" he exclaimed. "We thought that Waite had abandoned us. Guys, they've sent help!"

De Vries watched in astonishment as more people emerged from the tents into the clearing. They all clustered around him, reaching out their hands to shake his.

"Where are the rest of the team?" the man who had come out first asked.

It took De Vries a moment to get over his bewilderment.

"About that…"

***

"How do we stop the generator from overloading?" Alexa asked as another rumble shook the building.

"We need to shut down the power," Waite said, "but it's a very complicated process. I can't explain it to anyone that doesn't at least have a basic understanding of physics."

"I don't suppose Newton's Laws count?"

Waite shot her a bemused look. She chuckled. It was quite easy to rile him up. He reminded her of one of her old boyfriends that she'd had as a teenager. From back before her taste in partners had improved.

"How do we open up the building?" she asked.

"That requires going to security HQ, I think. It's not my area. I'm more concerned about stopping the destruction of the city."

Alexa glanced at the number on the wall as they passed another floor. They were only four levels away from the ground floor. They picked up their pace, Alexa in the lead with the rifle.

"How do we get to the basement?" she asked.

The stairs ended at the ground floor.

"Service stairs. Door behind the reception desk."

Alexa nodded. She pushed the doctor back against the wall. She slung her rifle and drew her sidearm. Keeping the weapon at the ready, she used her free hand to push the door open.

Beyond was what was once a fancy reception area. Except now it was a mess. Broken glass was everywhere. Various personal items were strewn about, from makeup cases to phones. It looked like a stampede had been through. And amongst the rubbish were the dark brown stains of dried blood.

She pushed the door all the way open and stepped out into the lobby. The harsh glow of the emergency lights gave everything a hellish, ethereal quality. But it was clear. She called to Waite to join her.

"Where is everybody?"

Waite shrugged. "I don't know what security told them. Probably holed up somewhere. Come on, woman! We don't have much time."

As they were jogging across the floor, a loud, metallic banging sound stopped them in their tracks. Alexa spun towards the sound, rifle up and ready. It was coming from one of the elevators.

She moved up to it carefully. The banging continued. It was deliberately spaced out. Almost like a code.

"Who is it?" Alexa called.

"Santa fucking Claus," came Monroe's voice. "Get me the fuck out of here, Rojas."

***

"Three floors left," Janelle said.

"Awesome," Teller said through gritted teeth. "Just a couple more minutes of intense agony."

"On the bright side, at least your boy is going to love your dino stories."

"Nah. He prefers cars. My little girl, on the other hand. Bought her every dinosaur book there is. She knows all their scientific names."

"Smarter than her daddy then?"

"Oh, by far. I can't even pronounce half those damn names."

"Hey, if either of us had any brains, we wouldn't be here right now."

"Fair point."

Once they reached the basement level, Janelle set Teller down on the final flight of stairs. He grunted as his backside hit the step.

"How we gonna do this?" Janelle asked.

"You leave me here, is how," he replied. "No way you can carry me through a hazardous environment. The LT and De Vries are sure to have made it by now."

"Hopefully."

"Need more than a couple of dinosaurs to kill those two tough old bastards, I can tell you that for free."

Janelle held out her hand. "It's been a pleasure."

Teller shook it. "All mine, Marine. Don't get killed. I want you to meet my kids."

"Roger that."

CHAPTER 30

"We were the first team sent through the portal," the scientist said to De Vries. "We came through with equipment, supplies, and a security team two weeks ago. The portal shut down after we were through. We've heard nothing since."

"Waite made no mention of you and yours," De Vries said. "Something went wrong. His machine has been opening portals like crazy, sending all kinds of *kak* into your offices."

"We noticed the portals opening and closing. Some of them seem to keep popping up nearby, depositing debris and..." the man shuddered, "...bodies. We thought that they were trying to get through to us."

"Waite wants to shut them down. Only way we're gonna get out of here is if we ride one of the random ones back."

"I was afraid of that. It won't be easy. We can't predict them, you see. Only warning we get is the rumbling."

"How many people have you got here?"

"Seven. We lost a few on our first night. Raptors, I think. But they seemed to stop coming after a while. Something about the portals keeps them away."

"Get everyone together," De Vries said, standing. "We need to be ready to jump through the first portal to open. My team is trying to shut these things down and if they do, I don't think anyone else is going to come for us."

"I'm not sure we can. We're tired. Worn out. Living here has taken its toll. We weren't built for it."

"Look, my friend. I know you've had it hard. But if you and yours don't get a *fokken* move on, you're gonna be stuck here for a lot longer. Stop whining, get off your arse, and gather your people. We don't have much time."

De Vries hoisted the man up by his shirt. "If you're giving up, now is the time to tell me."

The scientist looked into his eyes for a moment before eventually shaking his head. De Vries nodded and let go of his shirt. The man hurried off to gather his team. Once he was out of sight, De Vries' shoulders sagged.

He was beyond tired. The old joke about being too old was playing in his head. Only it wasn't a joke. His bones were protesting, his joints screaming, and his muscles aching.

Outside, he heard excited voices as their leader told them the plan. It was probably the first speck of hope that the small group had had in a long time. De Vries wondered whether he had the strength to help them get home.

He didn't have much of a choice. Either he did his best or they'd resign themselves to starving to death in this bizarre forest. It was better to die trying to accomplish something than to give up and waste away.

De Vries took several deep breaths, straightened his back, and stepped out into the clearing. The entire team was standing outside, their eyes locked on him. They weren't carrying any bags, but had bottles of water hooked to their belts. Their faces told him that they were well and truly done with the world they'd found themselves in.

"Right then," De Vries said, "let's get you home, shall we?"

The group smiled and followed him as he retraced his path towards the massive pile of rubble. He had no idea how long they'd have to wait for the next portal or even if they'd be able to enter it once it appeared. But he just hoped that his tired old body would hold out long enough to make an attempt to get these people home.

***

Janelle stepped through the stairwell door and into a rainforest. At first, she was confused, feeling like she'd stepped through a wardrobe into a different world. But then she noticed that the vines and vegetation around her was wrapped around concrete pillars and metal pipes. She was in the right place. It's just that a jungle had grown in the basement since she'd last been in it.

From within the dense vegetation came the sounds of animals and insects. The place was humming with life. Growls, titters and squeals echoed through the newly formed jungle.

Janelle looked around, straining to see through the dense foliage. Even with the bright lights on the ceiling that were somehow still functioning, she couldn't see more than a few feet in front of her. The rifle in her hands, once so big and comforting, now felt like a small and useless thing.

Another rumble started. The jungle came alive as the animals within were disturbed by the shaking. A fine layer of dust fell from the ceiling.

She looked up. A crack zig zagged its way through the concrete, starting just over her head and disappearing into the canopy beyond. It wasn't long before the building gave way and came down on top of her. She wondered whether that would stop the explosion.

It didn't matter. Either way, Janelle had a job to do. Get to the generator and shut it down. She brought the rifle up and started forward. It was do or die time.

CHAPTER 31

"A full jungle," Monroe commented, "in a basement. In Manhattan. And I thought my day couldn't get any weirder."

"We saw one upstairs," Alexa said.

"Fascinating," Waite interjected. "It's like being this close to the power source has somehow accelerated growth. There seems to be an entire eco-system in here. Even more complete than it was upstairs."

"Awesome," Monroe said, "but how about we stop this thing going nuclear before we start studying the flora and fauna, eh?"

Waite nodded. "Of course. It should be that way."

He pointed through the thicket.

"Where's De Vries?" Alexa asked.

"He fell through a portal," Monroe replied. "Is there any way to bring him back, Doc?"

"Maybe. *If* we can shut off the power and reset the system, I should be able to get control over the portals once more. Then we can see about bringing your friend back."

"A slim chance is better than none. I'll take point. Rojas, cover our asses. Doc, just stay between and keep your eyes open."

Everyone nodded. Monroe started through the jungle, marvelling at how thick it was. Vines snaked around pipes and hung from branches. Trees sprouted from the concrete floor and walls. Water dripped steadily from leaves overhead. Insects buzzed around their heads.

There was something going on that was beyond Monroe's understanding. But whether it was science or magic, he didn't give a damn. De Vries was stuck god only knew where and it was his job as team leader to try and get him back.

In the rear, Alexa's eyes kept glancing at Waite. Something was bothering her. And it wasn't just the man's cowardice or casual sexism either. There was something else going on. Her cop instincts were going into overdrive trying to figure out what.

***

"Always thought I'd go out different," Peanut rasped. "Blaze of glory, you know?"

"You ain't done yet, brother," Ashan said.

A smile spread across the man's ashen face. "You and I both know I am. So you go ahead and help the others. Take Lizzie with you. Ain't no use staying here with a dying man."

"I'm not gonna leave you here, man."

"You… don't have a choice…"

Peanut's voice trailed off as his head slumped to the side. Ashan felt his own chest tighten in grief. He felt for a pulse and found none. He felt a hand on his shoulder.

"I'm sorry," Lizzie said.

Ashan took a deep breath. He stood up and turned to Lizzie.

"We have two choices," he said. "We stay here, or we go and help the others. The latter puts you in danger and will get me in trouble with Alexa and Monroe."

"I can see what you need to do." Lizzie bent and retrieved Peanut's sidearm. "Because I need to do it too. I don't trust Waite to be in charge of our lives."

Ashan nodded. With one last look at the body of his friend, he pushed open the door and started for the stairs to the basement, Lizzie following close behind.

***

Waiting had never been Teller's strong suit. He'd hated it for as long as he could remember. Whether it was waiting for his mom to get home from work at night or waiting for his kids to be born, he always found it uncomfortable.

It was no different now. In fact, it was worse. Sat on the step in the stairwell, his leg screaming and throbbing at him made him feel worse than he had all day. It wasn't just the pain, either. It was the feeling of being completely useless.

Teller let out an exaggerated sigh. The silence of the stairwell seemed to be closing in on him. Urging him to move. To do *something*.

Not for the first time, he cursed his broken leg. He cursed his pain receptors. He cursed his slow healing abilities, wishing he was like one of those heroes in the movies his kids liked so much. Impervious to damage and able to get over broken bones and gunshot wounds like they were nothing.

After he was done cursing, he started to think. He cleared his mind of self-pity and blame. He looked around. And got an idea.

CHAPTER 32

The rumbling was getting worse and more frequent. Leaves fell from the branches above. Birds and insects voiced their displeasure.

"We must hurry," Waite said.

They were all sweating. The jungle was thicker than they had thought, the heat borderline unbearable. As they hacked their way through, Monroe couldn't shake the feeling that something was watching them from the shadows. He kept catching movement in his peripheral vision.

Alexa had said nothing, but Monroe had noticed her body language. She knew. The set of her shoulders, the way she moved, it all told him that she knew of the dangers following them.

Waite did not. He seemed so caught up in the moment that his previously cowed, cowardly demeanour had fallen away. For the first time that day, Monroe could see why this man was so respected as a scientist. When in his element, the confidence of the fellow showed through.

Another rustle of the leaves. Monroe turned on his heel, bringing his weapon to his shoulder. The bushes swayed.

"We don't have time for this," Waite said.

As if to emphasise his point, the building shook once more. Monroe felt the concrete beneath his feet reverberate, the sheer energy causing cracks to appear in the parts of the walls that could be seen through the bush.

"Go," Monroe said.

"We're not going to leave you behind, Lieutenant," Alexa said.

"Yes you are. Waite is right. We don't have time. I'll catch up. Go!"

Alexa made a noise that was halfway between a swear word and an unintelligible sound of exasperation, but she nodded. She grabbed Waite and they kept going, crashing through the bizarre jungle. There was no time for stealth now.

Monroe kept his eyes forward. He swept his rifle from left to right, then right to left. He strained to hear anything unusual through the cacophony of rattling concrete foundations and jungle sounds.

He had no idea how big the basement was. Pipes, sweating and hissing, snaked their way through the trees. Big black generators and other equipment of suspect use stood silently, vines clinging to them, insects crawling this way and that along their metallic forms.

It was all so incongruous that it made his head hurt. The juxtaposition, the idea that such a thing could be possible, and the constant threat, was swirling around in his mind. And something was crashing through the undergrowth towards him.

Monroe steadied his breathing and took aim. It was getting closer. His finger drifted to the trigger, ready to squeeze at a moment's notice.

Something tumbled out of the bushes in front of him. The lieutenant was a split-second away from shooting it when he realised that it was Janelle.

"Jesus Christ, Marine," he breathed. "I almost blew your fucking head off."

Janelle gave him a look. "Maybe if you were a better shot, sir."

He smiled. "Where's Teller?"

"Someplace safe. I thought you could use the help. But sir, I feel like–"

"Something's following you? Yeah, I feel the same. You see anything?"

"More a hair on the back of my neck type situation, sir."

They both scanned the jungle. Monroe wished that the damn building would stop shaking so that he could hear properly.

"The others?" Janelle asked.

"We're covering their flank, Marine."

A branch cracked to their left. Janelle whipped around. Whatever was hunting them, it was getting closer. But what was it waiting for?

"Get ready," Monroe whispered, "it's coming."

***

"How are we going to find them in all of this?" Lizzie asked.

Ashan considered the question. They'd been trying to decide on a direction for almost ten minutes. Their first choice had gotten them turned around somehow, taking them straight into a dead end. The body of a maintenance worker lay at the end of it, his guts spilling out of a great gash in his stomach.

It would be no use to just wander in random directions. Especially when it looked like there were hostile creatures hidden amongst the thicket. The SEAL wished that he'd taken a picture of one of the maps upstairs.

Ashan was about to suggest a course of action when fate intervened. The sound of gunfire erupted out of the jungle, followed swiftly by a chorus of snarls, and yelling.

"We have our answer," Ashan said.

They took off running.

CHAPTER 33

The raptors struck without warning, exploding out of the undergrowth in a shower of leaves and broken twigs. They were all teeth and claws and death, heading straight for their target – Janelle.

Monroe's instincts and muscle memory took over. His brain had no time to think. He just reacted, his finger squeezing the trigger and sending hot lead towards the leaping raptor. It hit the creature centre mass, sending it crashing sideways, leaving behind a fine red mist and floating feathers.

He didn't stop to see it fall, instead adjusting his aim to acquire another target. He didn't get to do so. A pain so hot, so sharp, and so all-encompassing shot through his body, forcing a scream from his lips.

Janelle was screaming too, but Monroe couldn't hear her over the pain. It overtook all his senses, overloading his brain. Stars exploded in front of his eyes, great bursts of multi-coloured light that had no real shape.

Through the din, Monroe heard the dull sound of someone screaming. It was him.

He looked down at what was happening to his side. The sight horrified him. A raptor had clamped down on his thigh. Blood was everywhere, gushing out in great streams and spurts.

Monroe tried weakly to hit the thing, but his body wasn't having it. The thing was yanking its head back and forth, trying to tear a great chunk of flesh.

Gunfire erupted out of the jungle. Ashan and Lizzie had joined the fray.

The creature's neck exploded in a terrific display of crimson, its body separating from the head almost immediately. It fell to the floor, the legs kicking out and catching Monroe's shin. He tumbled over, hitting the ground hard.

There was more yelling. More gunfire. Shell casings flew in an arc through the air, bouncing off tree trunks and leaves.

Monroe saw it all happen in strange slow-motion, the sight of the casings and the muzzle flash glinting off of them strangely beautiful.

"I'm out!" Janelle cried.

She dropped the rifle to the ground and snatched at Monroe's, which lay next to him. It was then that she noticed that he was still alive.

The rifle forgotten, Janelle had to recall her battlefield medical training from years before. Monroe's eyes were open but glazed over. His mouth hung slightly open.

Ashan was choosing his targets carefully. He was down to his last two magazines. Meanwhile, Lizzie was just doing her best to shoot straight.

It was only when her rifle clicked on empty that she realised it was over. Blood splattered everything. It dripped slowly from the leaves of the trees and pooled on the ground underneath the bodies of the dead raptors. Her heart thudded so hard in her chest that she could barely hear anything else. It was not until Janelle grabbed her by the shoulder that she realised she was needed.

Monroe's skin was pale. A fine sheen of sweat coated it. His eyes were glassy and unfocused. His voice a mere whisper.

Lizzie attended to his wound. It was a mess. A great big, ragged gash on his thigh, as if someone had been hacking at it with a machete. She could barely see through the blood and torn scraps of flesh. She looked at Ashan hopelessly.

He was holding his lieutenant's hand in his. The man's grip was weak. A mere shadow of what it had once been.

"Fucking…" Monroe gasped.

"It's all good, sir," Ashan said. "We'll patch you up and have you back in no time."

"Bull…" the man coughed, "…shit. Your team."

Both Janelle and Lizzie were at a loss. The raptor's teeth had not only shredded flesh, but arteries and veins as well. The flow of blood was slowing. There was nothing they could do.

Ashan kept hold of Monroe's hand. He watched, his heart breaking for his brother in arms, as the light faded out of the lieutenant's eyes. It didn't take long. His hand fell from Ashan's.

"I'm sorry," Lizzie sobbed. "There was nothing I could–"

Ashan put a hand on her shoulder. "Nothing anyone could have done."

He started to go through his CO's pockets, grabbing all the ammunition that he could. He handed Monroe's pistol to Lizzie. Janelle helped her to her feet before grabbing the rifle she'd dropped earlier.

"We don't have time to mourn. We have to move."

"Come on, Doc," Janelle said softly. "Just put one foot in front of the other."

Lizzie nodded weakly. After having gone her whole life without seeing anyone die in front of her, the day was beginning to get overwhelming. But both Ashan and Janelle knew that if she stopped to think, it would get worse.

Ashan took point, striding into the trees, following the path set by Alexa and Waite earlier. Janelle followed, gently urging Lizzie along in front of her as she went.

Behind her, something grabbed the leg of a still twitching raptor corpse and dragged it into the jungle with a satisfied growl.

CHAPTER 34

"This is it!" Waite exclaimed.

He was oblivious to the gunfire behind them, instead running up to the bank of computers in front of them. The whole thing was covered in vines and fallen leaves, which the doctor hurriedly swept aside. He did the same to the body of a security man that was slumped in one of the chairs. It flopped to the floor with an unpleasant squelch.

"Anything I can do?" Alexa asked.

"No!" Waite said. "You'd get in the way, woman. Now be quiet and let me work."

Alexa bit back a snarky remark. Instead, she turned to watch their six. The gunfire had stopped. She couldn't shake the feeling that they'd lost someone. The screams had told her that one of their party was definitely injured.

She checked her rifle. One magazine was all she had. Her sidearm was almost empty too. Dust fell from the ceiling. A falling leaf landed on her shoulder. She brushed it off absentmindedly.

Visions of her son played in her head. She tried to hold onto his smile, hoping it would give her the strength to survive this. As a single mother with a high-risk profession, she'd made sure that if she didn't come back, he was taken care of. But she didn't want him to grow up without her.

Alexa pushed those thoughts out of her head. She had a job to do. Any distractions could get people killed.

Something was coming down the path she and Waite had made through the thicket. She could hear the sound of snapping branches and heavy footfalls. Which was how she knew they were human.

"Friendlies!" came a shout from down the path.

It was Ashan. Alexa smiled when she saw him, Lizzie, and another woman emerge from the foliage. The smile faded as she noticed Monroe was missing.

"Monroe?" she asked.

Ashan shook his head.

"Why are you two down here? I left you upstairs with…" She trailed off.

"I'm sorry. We thought you could use the help."

"Is that you Lizzie?" Waite called. "Get over here! I need help."

Lizzie, still somewhat dazed, took a moment to respond. She shook her head to clear it and jogged up to the console.

"What do I do?" she asked and got to work.

"You the marine?" Alexa asked.

Janelle nodded. "Yes, ma'am."

"Good. Our job is to keep the dinosaurs off the doctors until they fix this thing. Got it?" Both Janelle and Ashan nodded. "Let's do this."

Behind them, Waite burst into a string of curse words.

"What is it, Doc?" Alexa called.

"We're running out of time!" he screamed back.

A violent tremor ripped through the building, throwing everyone off their feet. A massive crack zig-zagged through the floor and ceiling. Chunks of rock rained down upon Alex and the two soldiers.

Lizzie struggled to her feet. She reached the keyboard, watching the string of code that scrolled down the screen.

"Just switching it off won't work," she said as Waite stood beside her. "We need to shut everything down remotely first."

The older man was sweating, his eyes wide in fear. "I… don't know how."

Lizzie studied the code for a moment more. She grabbed Waite by the shoulder, turning him to look at her.

"Get over to the breaker box! Get ready to flip the switch when I tell you."

Waite nodded and hurried off. The air crackled with static electricity. Lizzie's hair was dancing about her head. From above came the sound of tumbling masonry.

Compys, weird flying creatures, and insects of all types were fleeing from the crack in the building. Alexa rose to her feet on unsteady legs. She could feel the floor reverberating beneath her. Concrete dust clogged her nose and threatened to choke her.

She felt it before she saw it. A portal opened in the middle of the crack, small at first, but it expanded more rapidly than any other she had seen that day. It wasn't long before it was big enough to go from one end of the room to the other. It crackled and fizzed, letting off discharges of energy that burned whatever it touched.

As Ashan was just getting to his feet, a beam of blue lightning shot out of the portal, hitting him square in the chest. It threw him backwards with tremendous force. He hit the railing just behind Lizzie with a clang and thumped to the floor in a smoking heap.

Janelle was already moving towards him. Another shot of energy hit the floor just in front of Alexa, leaving it blackened and smoking.

As Alexa watched the shimmering, crackling portal she took a step back. It was still expanding, still growing larger by the second. She had no idea how big it was, but it was likely that it was a few stories tall.

Her mind was racing. She felt useless, unable to help the scientists behind her. All she could do was stand, watch the thing in front of her grow, and fear what would come out of it.

"You may want to hurry up, Lizzie!" Alexa shouted.

"Almost there!" Lizzie called, desperately typing away on the keyboard.

She was remotely turning off the various machines throughout the building that were powering the portal generator. Behind her she could feel the build-up of energy. It was an oppressive weight on her back, so much so that she had to fight the urge to look. Her skin was tingling unpleasantly, her hair still standing on end. An eerie blue glow illuminated everything in the basement.

At the breaker box, Waite stood, his mouth agape at the spectacle. It was incredible, the culmination of all his years of research. Everything he had ever worked and lived for. He felt a sense of pride grow in his chest, despite all the carnage that had occurred.

Alexa took a few steps backward as the floor in front of her disappeared into the portal. A massive block of concrete hit the floor beside her, spewing up a great cloud of dust. She coughed, spluttered, and choked, looking up. She leaped backwards just in time as another jagged piece of masonry landed with a terrific crash.

Lizzie finally shut down the last machine. Sweat was pouring off of her forehead now. It splattered against the console in great rivulets.

"Now!" she called to Waite.

He didn't seem to hear her. He was transfixed by the sight of the portal. His creation. His achievement. It was so beautiful.

Lizzie didn't bother calling him again. She just took off at a dead sprint towards the breaker box. She barrelled into Waite, throwing him aside. Before he'd even hit the ground, she'd grabbed the switch and pulled it.

The basement lights went off immediately, followed seconds later by the computer consoles. Soon, all that was left was the blue glow of the portal.

Lizzie looked towards it, thinking that it was too late. That it wouldn't close. But then she noticed that it was shrinking, retreating into itself with each passing second. Then finally, it fizzled out in a last burst of static.

Only then did Lizzie breathe out. She collapsed to the floor in a heap, her body suddenly sore and weary. Alexa turned to her with a smile on her face.

"Good job, Doc," she said.

Lizzie returned the smile. She was about to speak. To say something about it all being over. But that's when the gunfire started.

CHAPTER 35

Once the rubble had stopped falling, De Vries started pushing the group through. There was no time for caution. He felt it in his bones that this was their last chance.

The portal was the biggest one yet. A huge ball of blue energy that crackled and fizzled with an intense energy of the kind De Vries had never seen. It was awe-inspiring, and would have stopped him in his tracks – if the sense of danger wasn't overtaking everything else.

As he counted the people jumping through the portal, De Vries hoped that they weren't landing on something dangerous. Water was pouring out of the portal, soaking through the old hunter's clothes. He shivered as the wind picked up. His leg was almost completely useless now. It hurt to stand.

The head scientist was the last one through and showed no hesitation. De Vries followed soon after, trying his best to ignore the pain in his leg. It turned his leap into more of a fall through.

There was a moment of weightlessness as he fell through, the energy enveloping him, charging through his body and making his skin tingle. Then he was out in open air again, the familiar smell of a crowded city filling his nostrils. Gasoline, oil, sweat, food, concrete dust.

De Vries landed with a thud, a jolt of agony shooting through his body. He cried out. Seconds later, several scientists were pulling him back from the still expanding portal. He noticed that some were crying, relieved to be back home at last.

They propped De Vries up against a car and began to fuss over him, making sure that he was alright. He let them do it. He was just happy to have a chance to sit down at last, and used his opportunity to take in their surroundings.

The portal had opened out onto the street directly in front of Starling Labs. It was deserted, the police cordon still in effect. The portal itself had enveloped a large portion of the front of the skyscraper. It was at least 20 stories high by that point and still growing.

De Vries hoped that the others were close to shutting down the power. It would be a cruel twist of fate if they had just got back home only to be vaporised by a massive explosion.

All eight of them were watching the portal now, transfixed by its undeniable beauty. It was a wonder of science, a miracle happening directly in front of them. Something that no one was likely to ever see again. De Vries figured it was a good enough sight to die watching. Yet he was forced to admit to himself that if it hadn't been, he was too tired and sore to care.

Despite the spectacle, all he wanted to do was sleep. Drift into a deep black abyss and give his body time to heal itself. Give his medication a chance to work at last. He knew in his heart that he couldn't, however, because he was the only one who could get these scientists to safety.

He started to shout at them to run. To get as far away as they could. The team leader echoed the order and one by one they reluctantly left, some saying thanks and patting the old man on the shoulder before they did so.

Only the head scientist stayed. He took a seat next to De Vries, who was too worn out to argue.

And so they sat and watched the portal as it grew. It was devouring the skyscraper, eating more and more of it as it went. Glass shattered, concrete tumbled, rebar clanged to the pavement. A great cloud of dust gave the scene an otherworldly quality as it hovered in the air like fog on a chilly night. The orange glow of twilight made it seem even more unreal, as the sun dipped below the massive skyscrapers that made up Manhattan.

The portal continued to expand. It shimmered, wobbled and shook, until finally, it seemed as if it was shrinking. It took De Vries a moment to notice, but once it started in earnest it was obvious.

He was about to cry out in happiness as an intense feeling of joy threatened to overwhelm him, when a massive foot stepped out of the portal and onto the pavement. It was swiftly followed by the rest of the creature, which was all muscle and teeth.

The dinosaur's tail just made it through the portal before it closed behind it. It stood for a moment, taking in the new sights, sounds, and smells that were so alien to it. And its two hungry eyes settled on the only prey it could see.

CHAPTER 36

De Vries knew what he needed to do. His rifle was beside him, his hand already on the grip. He had to raise it and fire. Put as many rounds into the tyrannosaurus rex's head as possible. If he didn't, he and the scientist were both dead. It was that simple.

So why can't I do it? he thought to himself.

His hand would not move. His body would not react. He was completely and utterly spent. Not frozen in fear, not shocked stock still. In fact, he felt nothing except a deep, almost profound sense of fatigue. It felt like he'd given all he had to give.

Even the sight of the most awesome dinosaur he'd ever seen couldn't get him to move. It was almost absurdly large, its head easily bigger than most men. Its teeth were long and razor-sharp, its eyes glinted with an animal intelligence that most carnivorous hunters had. The body itself was long, sloping elegantly into a massive tail. The legs were gigantic slabs of muscle with great feet designed to support the obscene weight of the creature.

The T-Rex eyed the small things in front of it. Underneath its feet was a texture it had never felt before. Rough, hard, uncomfortable. A cavalcade of different smells were assaulting its senses. Nasty, unnatural scents that the creature couldn't decipher. The sounds were worse – they hurt its ears as they shrieked and jabbered.

But the things it looked down at were living, breathing creatures of some sort. *They* smelled good. Like flesh, blood and food. And the big creature was hungry.

It was about to eat them. De Vries knew it. He saw the body ready itself to bend, saw the jaws open. It was all about to end.

The spell was broken by gunfire. A quick volley of shots came from behind the creature. It straightened immediately, letting out a roar of pain that shook De Vries to his insides. Someone was shooting a handgun at a T-Rex.

The head scientist had snapped out of it. He was grabbing De Vries, dragging him to his feet. The hunter's body started to obey. Slowly, reluctantly, he stood, trying to will life back into his limbs.

"Run," he said.

"I'm not leaving you!"

The gunfire continued. More bullets slammed into the thick hide of the creature. It turned towards the thing that was biting it. It saw another one of the small animals. This one was making flashes happen with its hands. It stood awkward, as if injured.

Teller's handgun clicked on empty. He ejected the magazine and slammed a fresh one home in one smooth movement. He was pulling the trigger as the empty clattered to the floor. The dinosaur was advancing towards him now, its great jaws opening as it let out a terrible roar.

He couldn't run or move. His leg made sure of that. Even the makeshift crutches that he'd fashioned out of two mops could only get him so far. But he was giving De Vries and the other man time to get away, and that was all that mattered.

***

The sight that greeted them after they had navigated the broken building and gotten back to the ground floor stopped Alexa and the others in their tracks. Even after all they'd experienced, the image of the massive dinosaur standing in the middle of Downtown Manhattan was still awe-inspiring.

It was Ashan who brought them to their senses. He was burned and bruised. Janelle was holding him up, his arm over her shoulder. He noticed that it was Teller who was doing the shooting. The creature was heading straight for him.

Without thinking, he raised his rifle and fired one-handed. A quick burst of semi-automatic fire caught the animal in the thigh. A fine mist of blood sprayed as soon as the bullets hit. The T-Rex stopped in its tracks, its massive head turning towards this new threat.

"Get inside!" Ashan said, pushing Janelle away.

He stood on shaky legs and continued to shoot. Most of his rounds went wide. Each shot brought a fresh jolt of pain as the rifle jarred his severely burned chest.

Someone was screaming, loud and shrill. Alexa and Janelle had both started shooting as well, aiming for the head.

Lizzie was trying to back up into what remained of Starling Labs. A good twenty stories and couple of feet had disappeared from the front of the skyscraper. Water gushed out of pipes and tumbled down from above. A three-foot-wide hole had been taken out of the floor. If they could just get into one of the back rooms, she and Waite would be out of the way.

But Waite wouldn't move. He was screaming, long and loud and shrill. Lizzie was pulling hard on his arm. He wouldn't budge. He was rooted to the spot.

There was a sudden blur of movement beside Lizzie and Waite disappeared. A geyser of crimson blood, hot and sticky, sprayed over her soon after. At first, she had no idea what it was. She reached up to her face to wipe it off, staring at it on her hand in confusion. That didn't last long. She looked down to see Waite getting devoured by a massive Utahraptor.

Alexa heard the commotion behind her just as her rifle clicked empty. She discarded it and drew her sidearm before turning around. What she saw made her blood run cold.

The tail of the Utahraptor caught Lizzie in the stomach as it thrashed around in excitement. It knocked the air from her lungs and flung her backwards. She flew through the air for a good five feet before crashing into the wall. Her head took the worst of the impact, slamming hard into the concrete and knocking her senseless.

Just beyond the mess that had once been Doctor Waite and his killer were three more raptors, their teeth bared and a nasty glint in their eyes.

"On our six!" Alexa cried, firing her handgun in their direction.

Janelle was on her last magazine for her rifle. And none of her shots seemed to be doing more than angering the great beast that was now lumbering towards them. She heard Alexa's shout. She didn't hesitate.

Grabbing Ashan, she dragged him off to the side as the Utahraptors leapt forwards. Alexa did the same, diving sideways. She hit the ground and continued to move, crawling towards Lizzie's unconscious form.

The raptors sailed through the air, past their feasting fellow, and landed near the hole that led into the lower levels of the building. One misjudged the landing, slid forward, and tumbled over the edge to its death. But the others didn't care, because they now had a new threat.

One of the raptors jumped the gap and dodged around to the left of the T-Rex, which let out another roar of anger upon seeing predators that it recognised. It reacted on instinct alone as the third raptor tried to run around to its right, bending over and clamping its jaws on the writhing body of its foe.

The Utahraptor let out an ear-splitting shriek as the massive jaws of the T-Rex clamped down onto its body. It found itself lifted in the air and violently shaken from side to side, spraying its blood across the pavement and windows of the surrounding buildings. The shriek was cut short as the creature's neck broke, causing it to go limp in the T-Rex's jaws.

Meanwhile, the raptor that had dodged left snapped at the leg of the T-Rex, ripping out a chunk of flesh. The beast roared once more, dropping the body of its conquered foe and turning to this new threat.

The Utahraptor that had been feasting on Waite raised its head at the commotion. It saw what was happening to its pack and leapt into action.

"Lizzie, are you okay?" Alexa asked. "Lizzie!"

Lizzie's eyes were open, but her gaze was unfocused and distant. Blood was smeared on the wall behind her. Alexa checked the wound. Lizzie's hair was matted with blood and there was no way to tell how bad the damage was.

Janelle had gotten to her feet. She was dragging Ashan back into the building, trying her best to get him out of the way of the terrific battle that was happening in the street. She almost slipped in the blood that coated the floor and still flowed from Waite's corpse.

"We need to get to a vantage point," De Vries breathed.

The scientist had dragged him into the lobby of the building opposite. They were taking cover in the elevator lobby.

"Why?"

De Vries hefted his weapon. "Need to get a good shot."

The scientist looked about, his eyes settling on the stairs. De Vries nodded. The man hefted the old hunter up once more and they started for the stairwell.

"Name's Jake, by the way," the scientist said.

"Dante. Pleasure."

Now the T-Rex had two raptors to deal with. They were agile, fast, and almost impossible to catch. They danced and dodged around the bigger dinosaur, taking their pound of flesh whenever they had the opportunity.

One of them hopped up on the roof of a car and then leapt onto the back of the tyrannosaurus. It sunk its claws into the tough hide of the animal and began to use its teeth to inflict more damage. A great roar shook the surrounding area in response.

The last Utahraptor tried to capitalise on this opportunity. It didn't get the chance. The T-Rex used its gigantic head as a battering ram, sweeping it to the side and catching the raptor in its midsection. The thing was lifted off its feet and thrown through the window of the building opposite. It smashed through the glass in a shower of glinting shards.

Jake and De Vries were heading straight for the window when the Utahraptor crashed through it. It was a standard office, full of cubicles, computers, and papers. The thing smashed into one of these. Papers flew up into the air as it did so.

De Vries immediately dropped behind one of the cubicles, dragging Jake with him. He looked at the scientist and held a single finger to his lips. They could hear the creature thrashing around in pain, knocking over office equipment in the process.

The Utahraptor finally made it to its feet. From outside came the sounds of battle. Stomping, crashing, roars, and shrieks as its fellow and the T-Rex battled. But there was something inside the new place it had found itself in that was more interesting.

It sniffed the air, ignoring the strange scents coming from outside. Instead, it focused on the smell of adrenaline and sweat that it could detect inside. It was the smell of prey, and it was within reach.

CHAPTER 37

Teller's mind was racing. He'd seen Ashan and Lizzie go down, but he knew that he couldn't help them. His leg felt like it was on fire already. There was no way he could make it down to them.

From his position on the second floor, he had a clear view of the battle happening out in the street. The raptor was doing its best to hang onto the back of the T-Rex as it thrashed about. The beast's massive foot landed on the roof of a car. The vehicle pancaked almost immediately, the windows blowing out in a brilliant shower of glass.

His original plan had been to get to the security room while the others shut down the generator in the basement. That had been vetoed when the massive portal had almost swallowed both him and the room whole. He'd been forced to scramble up a flight of stairs to safety, broken leg and makeshift crutches making it the hardest thing he'd ever done.

But now there was only one thought in his mind. Stop the tyrannosaurus. They couldn't let it loose on the streets of Manhattan. It would cause too much destruction. He'd seen the movies with his kids, he knew how it would end. People would die. He couldn't let that happen. They needed backup.

Alexa had given up on trying to rouse Lizzie from her stupor. She'd grabbed the doctor by her shirt and dragged her back into the relative safety of the stairwell. She propped her up against the wall to examine her injuries.

The head wound had stopped bleeding, but that didn't stop Alexa from pulling a field dressing that she'd grabbed from Ashan from her pack. She pressed it against Lizzie's head and told her to hold it there. The doctor complied.

That gave Alexa time to take stock of her ammunition. It wasn't good. She only had one magazine left for her sidearm. There was no way in hell that that was going to cut it against the beast that was still roaring in fury outside.

The door to the stairwell burst open suddenly as Janelle kicked it open. She carried a groaning Ashan inside as Alexa shut the door behind her.

"How is he?" Alexa asked.

"Still alive," Ashan said, "barely. Chest hurts like crazy. Can barely stand. I might be out of this fight."

"And here I thought you SEALs were tough," Janelle said, sitting him down next to Lizzie.

"What's your ammo situation?" Alexa asked.

Janelle shook her head. "Not good, boss. I got one mag left for the rifle, then I'm out. Ashan's empty."

"I have this." Ashan held up a hand grenade. "Might come in useful."

Alexa took it from him. "It just might. Marine, with me. We need to get upstairs to Teller. See if we can make use of this."

In the street, the raptor was thrown clear of the Rex's back. It crashed through the glass doors of a building, sliding along the tiled floor and smashing into a security desk. The tyrannosaurus roared in triumph.

But the Utahraptor wasn't out of the fight yet. It got to its feet unsteadily, its claws unable to find much purchase on the smooth floor. Blood dripped from its mouth. Its beady eyes fixed on the creature outside and it snarled.

Meanwhile, De Vries and Jake could hear the raptor stalking them through the cubicles. It knew where they were. The old hunter knew it. There was no hiding from apex predators.

De Vries tapped Jake on the shoulder. He pointed to the opposite end of the room. With a series of gestures, he got his point across. The scientist nodded. De Vries counted to three with his fingers.

On three, Jake stood and took off in a dead sprint towards the other side of the room. The Utahraptor's head whipped up as its prey darted in front of it. It started after the scientist.

De Vries was already on his feet, leaning hard against the cubicle for support. His rifle was up, his eyes on target, his spirit willing, his body weak.

His aim wavered too much for his liking. Time was growing short. It would be on Jake in mere seconds. De Vries sighted and squeezed the trigger once, twice, three times.

The first shot went wide, shattering one of the windows that looked out onto the street. The second and third caught the creature mid-leap, throwing it sideways into a cubicle.

A quick look over at Jake told De Vries that he was okay. Then he was moving, heading straight for the window he had just accidentally shattered. There was no time to confirm his kill. He had to take out the T-Rex.

The raptor charged out of the building at tremendous speed. All human eyes would have seen would have been a blur of feathers shooting out of the broken glass doors.

It jumped as it ran, landing on the roof of a car, intending to leap from that to the neck of the T-Rex. But the roof of the car buckled, crushed under the incredible weight of the dinosaur. The raptor lost its balance and tipped sideways. Yet it still attempted its leap, still going for the kill.

From above, Teller watched the spectacle. His mouth dropped as the T-Rex took advantage of its foe's blunder, reacting at a lightning-fast speed that didn't seem possible for something that size.

The rex caught the Utahraptor in its jaws and clamped down tight. There was a terrible shriek, followed closely by rivers of blood that coated the pavement. The tyrannosaurus dropped the carcass of the raptor to the floor, put one foot on it, and roared.

One floor above the creature, De Vries took aim at its head through the open window as its roar rattled his bones. He was still unsteady, his aim still wobbling something fierce.

He rested his rifle on the windowsill and jammed the stock into his shoulder. He felt his finger go to the trigger, like it had a million times before. He sighted his target, took a breath, exhaled, and squeezed.

Janelle and Alexa arrived at Teller's side just as De Vries took the shot. Alexa saw the bullet hit the massive creature in the eye, stopping its roar short. She saw her chance.

"Grenade out!" she yelled.

She pulled the pin and tossed the fragmentation grenade towards the tyrannosaurus. The three of them hit the ground and covered their heads just in time.

There was a *whump* as the grenade detonated, forcing deadly shrapnel out in a spherical pattern from its point of detonation. This just happened to be underneath the chest of the T-Rex, which was almost instantly shredded to a fine pulp. The creature stopped moving almost immediately, before toppling forwards and landing in a bleeding heap on the street.

De Vries saw the beast fall. In his heart, he felt a dull ache at the loss of something so incredible, but he knew it was for the best. He didn't have time to contemplate the morals of his actions for much longer. He was swept off his feet as the Utahraptor that he thought he'd killed blindsided him.

His world was suddenly nothing but snapping jaws and rancid breath as the creature tried to take his head off. De Vries had just enough time to raise his rifle in defence.

The Utahraptor's powerful jaws snapped down on the weapon, almost snapping it in two. De Vries had to use all his strength to keep the thing from tossing the rifle aside and using him as a chew toy. Razor-sharp teeth snapping shut mere inches from his face, De Vries used the last ounce of strength he had to grope for his sidearm.

It wasn't long before the rifle snapped in half in a shower of springs and levers. The raptor swung its head violently from side to side, scattering the pieces everywhere in an attempt to get it out of its mouth. As it prepared to chomp down on De Vries' neck, the hunter finally got his sidearm out of its holster.

He didn't aim. He just pulled the trigger. Shot after shot after shot went into the Utahraptor's body. It didn't shriek or thrash or scream. It just died, almost in slow motion, the light going from its eyes before it collapsed to the floor.

De Vries lay on the floor next to it, covered in hot, sticky blood and panting hard. It was over. He could feel it, so he passed out.

CHAPTER 38

Three Weeks Later, Unknown Location

Alexa signed the document in front of her, pushed it across the desk to the guy in the suit, and sighed. Three weeks of intense debriefings and interrogation had resulted in a witness statement that the suits were happy with at last.

The guy took it and barely gave it a glance before shoving it in his brown manila folder. He nodded to her before leaving the room. She leaned back in the hard metal chair with a sigh. The moment of truth had arrived. Either they cleared her and the team or they didn't.

"You can leave now, ma'am," the suit said from behind her.

She started. She hadn't even noticed he was still there, holding the door open for her. That answered the question of whether they were cleared or not.

"Don't call me ma'am."

He blushed. A youngish guy, not very high up the chain. Alexa gave him a sympathetic smile.

"Where is my team?" she asked.

"Infirmary. The marine went there immediately after signing her statement."

Alexa nodded and thanked the guy. She knew where the infirmary was. She'd certainly spent enough time there these past few weeks. There'd been little else to do except watch daytime television. Not much entertainment when all your personal effects are confiscated for security reasons.

The infirmary was nothing more than a long, bare room with beds pushed up against the walls. Teller, Ashan, De Vries, and Lizzie were in adjacent beds, although Teller was the only one with a complex pulley system holding his broken leg up. Janelle was seated in a chair next to Lizzie.

"Are we finally through with this cloak and dagger shit?" Teller asked as Alexa walked into the room and grabbed a chair.

"All statements signed and sealed?" Everyone nodded. "Then it looks like we are. Although I think Lizzie will have to decipher a lot of the files that we pulled out of the Starling Labs computers for our science guys."

"When my head stops throbbing, sure," Lizzie said, gently touching her bandaged noggin.

"What happens now, hey?" De Vries asked. "We go back to our normal lives?"

"If you want to," Alexa said. "But we still have a few live specimens that we found in the building. They'll need studying and looking after. And you're the one with the most experience in the field at the moment, De Vries."

"Who the fuck are you, Rojas?" Ashan asked. "'Cause I've been thinking, the way this was handled, us being bundled here, everyone looking to you to answer questions. I assume you're not just a normal Fed."

"I can't confirm nor deny. Let's just say that my agency wasn't set up to handle normal crimes. Although I have to say that I did not expect things to get quite so crazy in there."

"Great. There's always someone up there pulling the strings, hey?" De Vries said.

"Afraid so. In this case, however, it is for the best. I took the liberty of making the recommendation that you are all transferred to my team on a more permanent basis. I hope you accept."

"*Jislaaik*," De Vries exclaimed. "Does this kind of crazy *kak* happen a lot then?"

Alexa smiled.

"You'd be surprised."

THE END

Check out other great

Dinosaur Thrillers!

Julian Michael Carver

TRIASSIC

After spending many years in artificial hypersleep, a handful of survivors of the exploration vessel Supernova awaken to find their ship torn to shreds. They are unsure of what happened in space or how they crashed into an uncharted planet. Upon exploration of the new world, they soon realize their destination: The Triassic, the first chapter of the Mesozoic Era. A plan is formulated to escape this terrifying landscape plagued with dinosaurs and prehistoric beasts. The survivors soon discover that there may be an even larger threat looming under the trees than just the dinosaurs, threatening to cut their mission short and trap them all forever in the primitive depths of the Triassic.

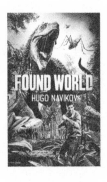

Hugo Navikov

THE FOUND WORLD

A powerful global cabal wants adventurer Brett Russell to retrieve a superweapon stolen by the scientist who built it. To entice him to travel underneath one of the most dangerous volcanoes on Earth to find the scientist, this shadowy organization will pay him the only thing he cares about: information that will allow him to avenge his family's murder. But before he can get paid, he and his team must enter an underground hellscape of killer plants, giant insects, terrifying dinosaurs, and an army of other predators never previously seen by man. At the end of this journey awaits a revelation that could alter the fate of mankind ... if they can make it back from this horrifying found world.

Check out other great

Dinosaur Thrillers!

Steve Metcalf

OBJEKT 221

Ruthless multi-national conglomerate Allied Genetics is under siege from a paramilitary force for hire. Allied calls in reinforcements and fortifies their crown-jewel property – an abandoned Soviet military facility in Crimea known during the Cold War as Objekt 221. Fortunately for the future of their research, O221 straddles a stretch of rocky landscape that hides a rift – a portal through time and space. Through this rift, Allied Genetics can travel, at will, to the Cretaceous – 100 million years into Earth's past – and bolster their genetic experiments with dinosaur DNA … something their competitors want to stop at all costs."Objekt 221" is a story blending numerous science fiction elements such as repurposed military facilities, time travel, rogue corporate armies, dinosaurs and the hint of a super-ancient civilization.

Bestselling collection

PREHISTORIC:
A DINOSAUR ANTHOLOGY

PREHISTORIC is an action packed collection of stories featuring terrifying creatures that once ruled the Earth. Lost worlds where T-Rex and Velociraptors still roam and man is now on the menu. Laboratories at the forefront of cloning technology experiment with dinosaurs they do not understand or are able to contain. The deepest parts of the ocean where Megalodon, the largest and most ferocious predator to have ever existed is stalking new prey. Plus many more thrillers filled with extinct prehistoric monsters written by some of the best creature feature authors this side of the Jurassic period.

Check out other great

Dinosaur Thrillers!

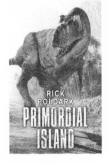

Rick Poldark

PRIMORDIAL ISLAND

During a violent storm Flight 207 crash-lands in the South China Sea. Poseidon Tech tracks the wreckage to an uncharted island and dispatches a curious salvage team—two paleontologists, a biologist specializing in animal behavior, a botanist, and a nefarious big game hunter. Escorted by a heavily-armed security team, they cut through the jungle and quickly find themselves in a terrifying fight for survival, running a deadly gauntlet of prehistoric predators. In their quest for the flight recorder, they uncover the mystery of the island's existence and discover an arcane force that will tip the balance of power on the primordial island. Things are not as they seem as they race against time to survive the island's man-eating dinosaurs and make it back home in one piece.

P.K. Hawkins

SUBTERRANEA

Fall, 1985. The small town of Kettle Hollow barely shows up on any maps, and four young friends are used to taking their BMX's outside of town in an effort to find anything interesting to do. But tonight their tendency to go off by themselves may have saved them, and also forced them into the adventure of a lifetime. While they were away, Kettle Hollow has been locked down by the government, and a portal to another world has opened on Main Street. It's a world deep below the ground, a world where dinosaurs roam free, where giant plants and mutant insects hunt for prey. It's also a world where all their family and friends have been kidnapped for sinister purposes. Now, with time running out before the portal closes, the four friends must brave the unknown to save their loved ones. Time is running out, and in the darkened tunnels of Subterranea, something is hunting them.

Made in the USA
Monee, IL
17 June 2021